About

Leeds born Eileen
German at Portsm(
crime novel, 'Miss
published by Robert ... .. 2010. It was taken up by Harlequin.com of California. Her second book, 'Blackmail for Beginners,' was published in 2012. Her third book, 'We'll be Watching You,' came out in 2013 and Harlequin immediately bought the paper back rights. She has just completed the sequel for 'Blackmail for Beginners,' in the 'Blackmail' series. The title is 'Sins of the Past.' and it should be out later this year. Eileen writes about ordinary people and puts them into extraordinary situations. She writes cosies with a dark edge.

Praise for 'Sins Of The Past'

Fresh from her triumphant sleuthing in 'Blackmail for Beginners' Miss Laura Windle is once more on the case in 'Sins of the Past.'

Eileen Robertson's cracking new novel is tense, tearful and rich in humour, and establishes Miss Windle in the pantheon of female detectives.

Julia Bryant. Saga writer.

Eileen Robertson's retro-mystery, 'Sins of the Past' inhabits a land far away from social media, techno-communications and the rule of sound bite. It is a 'Cosy' with a dark undercurrent – a story that spools out as casually as a fishing line in a trout stream, until it hooks you.

Laura Windle is a protagonist in search of the truth, but truth here is multi-layered and rarely what it seems.

Warmth, humour and a wry nod to English eccentricity, place 'Sins of the Past' firmly in the heart of trusted crime writing. A great read.

Pat O' Keeffe. Crime writer.

Suspicion runs rife in a quiet Yorkshire village when anonymous letters begin to arrive and a blackmailer means business. Can anyone be trusted?

Friends and neighbours shiver behind closed doors until, in a tense conclusion at a memorable dinner party, Eileen Robertson skilfully draws together the tangled threads in this traditional English village mystery.

Nicola Slade. Crime writer.

Sins
Of The Past

Eileen Robertson

Published 2015 in Great Britain
*Originally published as an ebook by
Endeavour Press Ltd, 2015.*

All rights reserved.
No part of this publication may be reproduced, stored in a retrieval system, or transmitted in any form or by any means, electronic, mechanical, photocopy, recording or otherwise, without prior written permission of the copyright owners. Nor can it be circulated in any form of binding or cover other than that in which it is published and without similar condition including this condition being imposed on a subsequent purchaser.

ISBN: 978-1519155757

British Cataloguing Publication data:
A catalogue record of this book is available from the British Library

Chapter One

November 1972
Monday 7pm

The man, smartly dressed in a business suit, stood in the shadow of the oak tree and watched the slight figure of Laura Windle hurry up the path towards the church hall. As the door closed behind her he got into his car and drove off. Time was short; he had work to do.

Reaching his destination he parked the car, pulled on his gloves, picked up his briefcase and walked down the path towards the house. He rang the doorbell, although he did not expect a response. Pausing only for a few moments he brought out a bunch of keys and a torch, and within seconds he had the front door open. He closed it behind him and allowed his eyes to become accustomed to the dark. Entering the living room he checked that the curtains were drawn, then made his way across to the writing desk. Soon he had the desk drawer open. Then he saw it. There it was, exactly as he'd been told. Carefully he eased the black ledger out of the drawer and laid it on the desk flap. Aided by the light of his torch he opened it and turned the pages back three years until he found the entries for 1969. Reaching into his briefcase he brought out his camera and fitted the flashbulb. Within minutes he had taken the photos and replaced the ledger where he found it.

Retracing his steps he went outside, locking the door behind him. All had gone well. He got into his car and smiled in satisfaction as he glanced once more at the house before driving off. To all intents and purposes, everything was as before.

*

The 'Preparation for Christmas' Meeting
7.30pm

Laura Windle sat on the front bench in the church hall, her shoulders hunched with cold, and tried not to fidget. Her mouth tightened as she glowered at the Reverend George Wilson, she didn't want to be rude, but sooner or later, something would have to be said. He had been told many times if there was to be a meeting it was always best to turn the heating on an hour before people arrived. One would think common sense would tell him that, she thought, but no, he had not listened. So here they sat in mid-November, all half-frozen, whilst the vicar rambled on and on about, of all things, good will and Christmas cheer.

The vicar's voice broke in on her thoughts, 'surely, Miss Windle, you of all people must have some Christmas tales to tell. We all have to make some effort for the Christmas party, perhaps you could recite a poem for us, or a reading from the Gospel?'

Horrified, Laura stared up at him. 'Oh no, Vicar,' she hedged, 'you see my voice is not quite what it was in the old days, and really...'

'Do come on, Miss Windle,' the vicar urged, with a hint of desperation in his voice. 'We're very short of volunteers, you've lived in Fawdon most of your life. You must have some interesting stories to tell.'

Laura suppressed a smile. Indeed I have, she thought, but you will not be the one to hear them.

'Really Vicar, I'm retired now. Yes, I do some work at the Children's Hospice and I try to help wherever else I can – in the Mother's Union and the Pensioner's Society, along with several other worthy causes. But as for reciting poetry,' she shook her head. 'There are other ladies far more accomplished in entertaining than I...' She shot a glance at the ample figure of Mrs Mould who was seated two places along from her, 'Mrs Mould for instance.' She knew this lady was always keen to sing and dance at any given opportunity.

The vicar hesitated as he glanced in Mrs Mould's direction. Laura could see that he didn't want to be rude, she watched as his face turned quite pink.

'Mrs Mould, would you be willing to, er, give us some entertainment during the festive season? A song? A carol? Or even a monologue?'

'Certainly Vicar,' Mrs Mould shuffled forward to the edge of the bench and beamed up at him, 'anything at all,' she said eagerly. 'I can dance quite well you know, just you say the word, Vicar, and I'll do it.'

Laura leaned back and watched the vicar's expression. Rumours travel fast in this village and judging by the vicar's pink face, she knew that he had heard about this lady's spouse – the miserly Mr Mould.

'I must say this is very good of you, Mrs Mould,' the vicar replied with some reluctance. He cleared his throat and said. 'And if you're quite sure your dear husband will approve?'

'Nah, don't you bother 'bout him, Reverend,' she tapped her nose, 'what he don't know can't worry him.'

Laura put her hand to her mouth at this remark. 'Oh dear,' she murmured, 'that is the understatement of the year.'

The vicar opened his mouth to reply to Mrs Mould's comment but then he appeared to have second thoughts. 'Well thank you, Mrs Mould, and of course all of you ladies, at least we've made a start on our Christmas plans. And please, please, if you can think of any more suggestions just contact me.'

By now all of the women were heading towards the door. 'You know where to find me,' he called after them. 'And remember, time is of the essence.' As Laura left she heard him announce forlornly, 'and I declare this meeting closed.'

Laura hurried out of the church hall and down the road towards her house. It was a good five minutes walk, but if she moved swiftly perhaps she could warm up a little. The wind was biting and sharp, and her arms felt numb, but then being on the wrong side of sixty her circulation was not as good as it had been in her youth. It was November now and Fawdon, being so close to the Pennines, could be bitterly cold at this time of year. Still, there was no sign of snow yet and if that held off until the New Year then at least the winter would not seem so long. She tugged at her coat collar in irritation and increased her pace; how very different the Reverend George Wilson was from his predecessor, her dear friend Arthur. Fawdon was not quite the same since he had moved to York. Her annoyance grew when she thought about the present vicar and she felt even guiltier about her own behaviour. She should never have volunteered poor Mrs Mould, not that *she* was the problem, but Laura had had dealings with Mr Mould before. Her mind went back to an illuminating incident that had occurred almost three years ago and she gave a wry smile. Mr Mould would be wise not to challenge her; he was not quite the puritan he appeared to be.

Laura reached her front door and fumbled with the keys for even though she was wearing gloves, her fingers were stiff with cold. As soon as she had the door open, she hurried into the welcoming warmth of the hall. Switching on the light she went into the living room to turn the gas fire up, she'd left it on low to keep the heat in, but it still did not seem all that warm. Perhaps she had left a window open somewhere? She checked the windows, but they were all closed as she thought. She sniffed the air, there was the faintest smell of perfume lingering in the room, but it was not the kind that she usually wore; it was more an aftershave sort of scent, but how could that be? She'd had no visitors today, and she rarely had male ones. She sniffed again and as she did, remembered that fateful night over two years ago when she'd returned to the house only to find the curtains off the hooks, the tablecloth on the floor and... she drew in her breath sharply and stared in the direction of the writing desk.

'Stay calm,' she told herself as she dashed over to it and made sure that it was locked. Just to be certain she unlocked it and sighed in relief when she saw that the black ledger was still in its place. Closing the desk she hurried out of the room and down the hall to check the back door; yes the bolts were still on; she would never make that mistake again.

Without warning, thoughts of her departed friend Julia flashed into her mind and her sense of guilt returned. She should never have been so severe with Julia, perhaps if she had been more gentle, more understanding, things might have turned out different? Laura sighed, then reached in her pocket for a hanky to wipe away a tear. 'You cannot alter the past,' she told herself firmly as she went into the kitchen, took off her coat and hung it up. Looking down she saw that her cat Snowy was still asleep in her basket and smiled, thank the Lord; everything was in order, just as she had left it. She started to prepare her supper, but as she filled the kettle her thoughts returned once more to Julia. She had better check out her empty house again tomorrow, as Heaven only knew when Julia's sister Claire would decide to move in. She could make a slight detour before going to the High Street, then she would visit Mr Mitchell, the florist, and order a Christmas wreath for Julia's grave. Yes, she thought, as she made her cocoa, that would be most appropriate.

Chapter Two

In spite of the next morning being crisp and bright, Laura's mood darkened as she approached Julia's old house in Westdown Road. It brought back so many memories of that bleak winter day at the cemetery in February 1970.

She recalled the small group of black-clothed people who had stood in silence surrounding her friend's last resting place. Among them, standing slightly apart, was a blond haired woman, who, Laura realized, must be Julia's youngest sister; and, if she remembered rightly, her name was Claire Forbes.

Laura had eyed her thoughtfully; she seemed oddly dressed for a funeral. Yes, she was wearing black, which was the correct thing to wear, but the pill box hat with its half veil and two black feathers sprouting from the back of it as if to take flight, would certainly be raising some eyebrows, to say nothing of the rather tight black suit, the fancy black nylons and the three inch heels upon which she tottered.

Later, at the wake, Laura had lost no time in introducing herself to Claire. 'I am Laura Windle, Julia's friend,' she'd said, 'you might well have heard Julia mention me.' She hesitated then said, 'I cannot tell you how sorry I am that this tragic accident occurred. You have my deepest sympathy; she will be greatly missed.'

'Not by me, she won't,' Claire had sniffed. 'Yeah, I'm her kid sister, but to be honest Miss, er, Laura, we've not spoken for fifteen years. The only thing I ever got from her was a Christmas card in 1968 and, oh,' Claire paused and stared hard at Laura for a second, 'she sent a birthday card and a Christmas card with a letter last December.' She gave a girlish giggle, 'I'm a Sagittarius y'see.'

Laura had felt uneasy; she had known that Julia and her sister did not get on, even though Claire was Julia's only relative. She remembered Julia referring to Claire as, *"the suicide blonde."* When Laura asked what that meant, she'd replied *"dyed by her own hand."* She had two divorces before she was forty and she still can't leave the men alone. But, thought Laura, the important question was, had Julia ever mentioned anything to Claire in her letter, about *her* 'little business?'

'Stop worrying,' she told herself sharply as she walked along, 'the past cannot be changed. Concentrate on the here and now.' She reached Julia's garden gate and looked up at the windows of the house. No sign of any breakages or heaven forbid, any vandals. But wait... Laura blinked hard as she opened the gate, before marching up the path to the front door. Her eyes had not deceived her; there were net curtains up at the windows. She looked closer then bristled with indignation. Not only were they not the plain net curtains which Julia would have considered tasteful, these nets were draped across the windows and tied with large pink velvet bows, like something out of a Hollywood cinema set. Laura took a deep breath; Julia would have been outraged.

She stood for a moment staring at the offending curtains. Claire must be in the process of moving in and she hadn't even bothered to tell me, even though I have written to her offering my help. She clicked her tongue in annoyance. But just to be certain she hurried to the back of the house and, standing on tiptoe, peered through the kitchen window. Sure enough, on the draining board she could see a large packet of 'Flash' cleaner, and there, in the corner, a mop and bucket. At this Laura felt a mixture of hurt and disappointment. Even though she still had a key to Julia's house in case of emergencies, now that Claire was moving in she could not enter it without her permission.

Right now she would have loved to wander through Julia's old house again, thinking over past memories, for there had been good times as well as bad. As she peered through the kitchen window at the empty room she wondered what had become of Julia's furniture. She felt sure Claire would have sold it, for, judging by the fancy curtains, it would not be to her taste at all. Surely though, Laura reasoned, Claire would have kept some bits for herself? There had been some boxes in the attic but they were all tied up with string and she had not wanted to pry. What had happened to Julia's personal things, her clothes, her beautiful shoes and handbags? Laura stopped short as she thought about the brown leather handbag that Julia had had with her on the fateful day of the accident. It reminded her again of that list of 'prospective clients' that Julia had waved in her face that same morning. Whatever had happened to it? Had the ambulance men picked it up and stuffed it into Julia's handbag? She could not remember. Not that it mattered now, no one who read it would be any the wiser about what it meant unless they had more details. She tried to reassure herself – that was all over and done with now.

'Back a bit, Alan, left, left, stop! You're there.' A man's voice called out loudly and Laura heard the sound of a large vehicle reversing and coming to a halt, followed shortly by van doors slamming.

'That must be the removal men,' she said and she went back down to the front of the house and stared up at the large van that was now parked at the gate.

The back doors of the van were open and two men were already inside sorting out the furniture. Pausing only to nod politely at the men and to cast a keen look at the contents in the van, Laura hurried on. No sign of Claire though; she could only assume that the removal men had a key.

As she walked along towards the main street she glanced at the block of offices on the other side of the road and thought about Alec French, who ran a wholesale stationary business there. The last she had heard about him was that he had taken Mary, his wife, on a world cruise so she could not expect to see them again before the spring. She frowned, had Mr French finally learned his lesson and become a reformed character? His attitude regarding the opposite sex had been commendable over the last two years, Laura pursed her lips, but everyone knew that a leopard never changes its spots. How long, she wondered, would his good behaviour last this time?

She was approaching the big house on the corner of the High Street when the door opened and Mrs Hedgley emerged, guiding a gentleman through the doorway. He was wearing a black coat and holding a white stick. Laura stopped and gave a little wave in Mrs Hedgley's direction, then focused on the man dressed in black. She had certainly not seen him before; he must be a stranger to the village. She looked again at the white stick and the satchel which he wore across his shoulders, and then she had it. Of course, he must William Smithson, the new piano tuner. Fred Leeming, the present piano tuner had mentioned his successor's name to her before he retired. So this must be the gentleman who had taken over the business. Laura hesitated, should she stay here and introduce herself? It would be a friendly gesture, but the question was by doing so might she be considered nosy? Whilst she stood pondering she watched the man tap his way carefully towards her. It was then that Laura noticed the baby walker that little Jennifer had left stranded in the path; the man was heading straight towards it. She drew in her breath sharply and was about to call out, when, to her astonishment the man stepped round the baby walker without the slightest hesitation and continued on towards the gate unperturbed. For a moment Laura gaped at the approaching figure. 'How very odd,' she remarked to herself, then deep in thought, she hurried on towards the High Street.

Chapter Three

Tuesday

Simon Mitchell, the florist, stood outside his shop and with a sense of satisfaction, gazed along the street. Things were looking up in Fawdon, the village was expanding and new houses were sprouting up all around the area. With Leeds and Bradford airport only a few miles north and the city of Leeds with its theatres, quaint Victorian arcades and huge department stores about six miles to the east, Fawdon was rapidly becoming a commuter zone. More and more businesses were opening up in the village; they even had an Italian restaurant just along the street. He touched his thickening waistline, over the last few years he'd sampled their cuisine many times and, in his opinion, it was always excellent. He'd heard that the proprietor of the Golden Rose Tea Shoppe was not at all happy about such fierce competition but then everyone knew that a bit of rivalry in business was health... or was it?

His gaze moved to the other side of the street, where, almost opposite his premises, an empty shop with a flat above it had recently been let. There were signs that the new tenants would soon be moving in. Rumour had it that this shop would sell fancy goods and trinkets, which was reassuring. However, Simon knew that these days, shopkeepers could sell almost anything. He scowled, but if they should start to sell flowers, there was definitely going to be trouble. He turned round to look at the beautiful display of flowers in his window and instantly felt better. Who could compete with that? Nevertheless he would love to know what stock the newcomers had, for he'd seen them moving stuff into the shop over the weekend. What if they should sell vases and plant pot holders and other sundries which he already stocked? He broke off, distracted by the trim figure of Miss Windle approaching. Instantly, as if on reflex, panic gripped him.

'Don't be an idiot,' he reproached himself, 'those days are long gone, you've done nothing wrong.' Nowadays, he always used the freshest flowers for his funeral tributes. He'd be a fool to make the same mistake twice and try to hide a few old blooms in amongst the wreaths. 'Anyway she might not be coming to see me,' he muttered, but he still felt uneasy. He darted back into his shop and headed behind the counter just in case. But, as he stood there waiting for Miss Windle's arrival, his thoughts strayed again to the shop premises across the road.

It was all very worrying; he would dearly love to see what stock they had inside that shop and, more importantly, at what price they would sell it. It was no use though; he'd just have to wait until they opened. A darker thought slid into his head. Then again, perhaps there was a way...

Chapter Four

Tuesday morning

Martha McPherson, the owner of the Golden Rose Tea Shoppe, sat in her office and stared at the mail that the postman had just dropped on her desk. There, on top of the usual stack of brown envelopes, was a white envelope with her name printed neatly on it. She knew what it was. It was another one of 'those'. She'd done something about the letters some weeks ago and she'd thought maybe it would end, yet still they came. She would have to open it, although she knew what the contents was. With a trembling hand, Martha tore open the envelope. Inside was a single sheet of paper, on it was the same demand she had read a dozen times.

"Leave £100 in an envelope at the shed door of the bowling green at 7pm on Friday."

She bit down on her lip, and remembering the instructions of Mrs Roberts, the private investigator she'd hired, fought back the urge to crush the paper. She eased it gently into its envelope and placed it in her handbag. She would give it to Mrs Roberts later.

Pushing back her fear Martha ignored the rest of the mail for the time being, they all looked like bills anyway, and she returned to her original task of checking last month's takings in her accounts book. As she did so, her despair deepened. Just as she expected, the Golden Rose Tea Shoppe's takings were down by 40%.

She shoved the book away and leaned back in her chair. What on earth was she to do? It seemed that trouble never travelled alone. She was being blackmailed and all because of one mistake she'd made in her past. Now, added to this, the business takings were down. She could not go on losing money and paying out like this. If Mrs Roberts failed to trace the blackmailer and she couldn't pay up, then she'd run the risk of exposure.

Her heart pounded at the thought. She would lose everything.

'Focus on your business,' she told herself firmly, 'here you know what the problem is, and this you *can* do something about.' She thought this through and knew that the root cause of her business troubles began when that Italian, Alfredo Lorenzo, had decided to open up a restaurant at the other end of the High Street a few years ago. At first she'd thought it would be all right, that he would only open in the evenings and that her business would not be affected, but since last July, that blasted foreigner had decided to do morning coffee as well. From the on, her trade had slowly dwindled.

When she had first heard the news about the Italian Restaurant opening in the morning, she'd smiled wisely and dismissed it as a one off novelty. She'd felt sure her customers would stay loyal to her. After all, when she'd first moved to Fawdon from Scotland and opened up the Tea

Shoppe four years ago the Fawdoners had welcomed her, and now the Golden Rose Tea Shoppe was a kind of home from home for a lot of them. She'd felt sure her customers would never desert her. How wrong she had been.

Martha propped her head on her hands and sighed; what was she to do? She got up, went through the kitchen to the staff entrance of the Tea Shoppe, nodded to the waitress on duty, and stood watching her customers.

Two elderly ladies were seated near the window drinking tea, they truly were regulars, they came every morning without fail, bought a pot of tea between them and stayed there until lunchtime, gossiping. Martha sniffed; not much money to be made from those two. Her gaze moved on, in the corner, close to the radiator, sat old Sam Jennings with his boxer dog, Jessie. Martha scowled; she didn't have anything against dogs but this one dribbled and every day the cleaner had to wash the floor once they'd gone. Two other couples were seated at separate tables, judging by the carrier bags near them, they'd spent the morning shopping and were having a cup of tea before making their way home. So then, seven customers in all. Hardly enough profit to pay for today's electric.

Deep in thought Martha returned to her office, she was so used to running a profitable business over the years that she'd become comfortable. She clicked her tongue, no, that wasn't the right word, she'd become complacent, and that was the honest truth. So now what? She'd already tried offering cocoa as a third option to her beverages, but within weeks her customers had told her with true Yorkshire bluntness that the cocoa "weren't right" that it "weren't same as t' Italian Fellas Hot chocolate."

So if she were to stay solvent she must think of something else. She thought about putting on lunches and high teas but her gaze drifted towards the 'overheads' column in her accounts book and her mouth tightened. That would mean buying a new cooker, a deep fat fryer, and hiring additional staff.

Her anger grew; she would have to deal with this. Never mind what the locals told her, she would check this out for herself. She got up, picked up a pencil and paper, pulled on her coat and marched through the Tea Shoppe and out onto the High Street. When she reached the Lorenzo restaurant she looked at the menu in the doorway and scribbled down the prices of the beverages; they were all slightly cheaper than the drinks she offered. Again she checked the menu and noted that the charges for food were all very reasonable. Thoughtfully, she walked back towards her own establishment, she could not allow this *foreigner* to take all of her trade. How long would it be before he decided to offer lunches as well? She would need to work quickly and her margins would be narrow, but the battle must begin. She would start serving lunches and cut profits to the bone, and if that didn't work... her eyes narrowed, there had to be more than one way to get rid of Mr Lorenzo.

Chapter Five

Simon watched Miss Windle close the shop door and walk back up the High Street. He smiled and let out a soft sigh of relief, there'd been no need to worry. All Miss Windle had wanted was to order a Christmas wreath for her departed friend, Julia Barnes, so there'd been no reason for him to panic. He checked the instructions in his order book then crossed over to his workbench and returned the book to the drawer. Out of the corner of his eye he saw the door that connected to his flat inch open and a chubby grey haired woman peer into the shop.

'Has she gone?'

Simon grinned; he was not alone in his awe of Miss Windle.

'You can come out now, Edna. Miss Windle's on her way to declare war on the butcher.'

'Thank the Lord for that,' Edna Thackeray said nervously as she came into the shop. 'Not that I've anything against the butcher, but there's something about that woman. I dunno, whenever I talk to her, I always start to stutter.'

'Never you mind. You're safe now, we're not likely to be honoured with another one of her visits until Friday at the earliest.'

'Good,' said Edna. 'I've just come to tell you I've popped a cottage pie in the oven for you, I'd some left-overs, y'see. Should be ready in half an hour, then I'll stand in for you while you get your lunch.'

'You're an angel, Edna. What am I going to do when you're gone?' He watched as a wary expression came over Mrs Thackeray's face. He knew something was troubling her but she wouldn't tell him what it was.

'Back in half an hour then,' she said quickly and bustled through the doorway.

Simon became thoughtful as the door closed behind her; he really would miss her when she left. She'd been an ideal lodger, more than that, she'd kept her room spotless and she'd cooked him God knows how many dinners, always claiming it was something that she'd whipped up from left-overs, but they both knew it wasn't.

When she'd given him her notice last week he'd offered to reduce the rent as he didn't want to lose her. But she'd insisted that was not the reason for leaving. It was mainly due to 'family matters,' she'd added mysteriously.

Simon was doubtful about this; thinking back he felt sure that something had changed Edna's attitude dramatically since the visit of the blind man in November.

It had been on a quiet Wednesday afternoon when the unexpected visitor had entered his shop. Simon recalled it vividly; he'd been about to sit down to read the morning paper when he'd heard the shop bell tinkle, immediately followed by the tap, tap, tapping of a stick.

On noticing that his customer was blind, Simon had hurried round the counter to assist him. The man, who was wearing dark glasses and had a bag strapped across his shoulders, had smiled pleasantly at the sound of his approach. He'd asked whether a Mrs Thackeray lived here.

Simon had guided him to Edna's room but the effect on her when she saw the man had been startling. 'Bill' she'd cried out and she'd gripped Simon's arm tightly. The man had moved towards her and Simon heard him whispering to Edna as they went back to her room. He remembered following them and hesitating outside her room, wondering if he should knock on the door to check if everything was all right. He hadn't done so, but thinking back he wished he'd got a glass and listened at her door, just to be certain.

It still troubled him when he remembered that incident. Since then he'd tried on a couple of occasions to bring up the topic of the blind visitor to Edna, but she always dismissed his questions and changed the subject.

Simon scowled; it bothered him that such a motherly soul like Edna should have reacted like that. What was the problem? There must be some way of getting at the truth. He walked back to his work bench to finish the funeral tribute that had been ordered, remembering Edna's fearful expression that fateful day. He was determined to find out what was wrong. Cutting savagely at a branch of conifers he thought about how he would do this. No one, even a blind man, should be allowed to frighten an old lady like that.

Chapter Six

Tuesday evening

Cynthia Roberts tottered into the kitchen, tossed her keys on the table, kicked off her high heels and then flopped into the nearest chair. That was the down side of being a self-employed private investigator, she thought. She rubbed her aching feet, it had been a long tough day.

After a couple of minutes Cynthia stood up and padded over to the fridge to retrieve some left-over soup. That, with a few chunks of bread would do for the moment, she was still awash with the coffee she'd drank at the office; she could eat something more substantial later on.

Having eaten, she cleared the crockery into the sink, then, with reluctance, opened her briefcase. As she pulled out the files she gave a tired sigh, she didn't feel a bit like working, but, as her Harry had always said, "Never put off until tomorrow what you can do today." Cynthia sat down, selected an orange coloured file and re-read the notes and the crumpled letters that Mrs McPherson had given her last week. They definitely had to take priority; this was blackmail on a very large scale. She stared at her notes in silence. She didn't really want to believe what they were telling her, but she'd traced the letters her clients had received. The envelopes all had the

Fawdon postmark on them. There was little doubt, the blackmailer lived here... somewhere in the village, maybe somewhere close by.

When Cynthia first realized this, thoughts of Miss Windle had swept into her mind and bitter sweet memories of her earlier years of living in Fawdon with Harry, her late husband, had returned. True, Miss Windle had blackmailed her because of her dark past but to be fair, Cynthia had reneged on her promises to contribute to the hospice, although it had been for a good cause. She had settled up with her and moved house to Shadwell on the other side of Leeds. But then Harry had... she quickly shut off that train of thought and swallowed hard, thoughts of her deceased husband were still raw in her mind, it was only a year since she'd said her goodbye's. 'Stop your snivelling woman, and don't be so soft,' she could almost hear Harry's voice growling.

Two years ago she'd got herself a job, trained as a private investigator and now she worked for herself. Harry would approve, she knew that. She'd decided that the posh bungalow at Shadwell had to be sold. She'd rented an office in Leeds and bought this little house. Cynthia smiled; it seemed that fate had intervened. She was back where she'd been happiest, here in the village of Fawdon.

She picked up the notes once more, stared at them and thoughts of Laura Windle came back into her mind. Could she be up to her old tricks again? She doubted it. Angrily she shoved the papers back into the folder. This was either sheer greed or envy. The awful thing was it could be someone she knew, someone she liked, someone she was friendly with. But then the question was, would they, for reasons of their own, be friendly with her knowing that she was now a P.I? One would think that any blackmailer would shy away from her, but not if they were confident, not if they were professional. They would assume she was too stupid to find them out. Cynthia smiled at the thought. True she liked to look glamorous, but that didn't mean she was daft. Her smile became a grin; in her earlier profession too many men had made that same mistake.

She forced her mind back to the present. She hated the idea of being suspicious of neighbours and friends, yet she'd accepted the contracts so the work had to be done. Now she must find the blackmailer. Was it a him? Or a her? Or could it be them?

With a sigh she returned the folders to her briefcase, she needed help and there was only one person in Fawdon who could give it. Cynthia knew it would take most of her courage, but she would have to do it. Tomorrow she would call on Miss Windle.

*

Wednesday morning

Cynthia got out of her car, locked it and paused to look down at the grey Ford Escort; how times had changed, gone was the shocking pink Mini car that she'd loved so well. Although it had broken her heart to part with it, the pink Mini had been totally unsuitable for her new job. The Ford Escort was smart and discreet, but even she couldn't deny that it was rather dull.

Taking a deep breath Cynthia turned, opened the gate and strode down the path towards Miss Windle's front door. As she reached it she hesitated and did a last minute check on her appearance; make-up subtle, green suit smartly tailored, shoes casual. She glanced down again at her feet, she was accustomed to wearing high heels in the office and these new flat shoes felt uncomfortable, but when she'd visited Miss Windle's home on one distant occasion she'd noticed the clean but very worn carpets and she'd remembered how she'd had to trip gingerly across the room for fear of catching her heels. She shook her head; she was not going to risk breaking an ankle this time. One final check on her hands, nail polish pale pink, so nothing too brash there. 'Now, remember why you're here,' she told herself. Determinedly she pressed the bell.

*

Laura checked her watch, smiled, and hurried to answer the door bell's summons. At least this young woman is punctual, she thought as she opened it. 'Ah! Mrs Roberts, please come in.' She ushered her through to the living room. 'Please do sit down near the fire; it is quite chilly outside, is it not?' She watched as Cynthia Roberts perched on the edge of an armchair. She is nervous, Laura thought, so she sat down opposite her and tried to put her at ease. 'I was so sorry to hear about your husband, my dear. He was such a hardworking man...' she saw Cynthia's lips tremble so she said quickly, 'but I am pleased to hear that you are now so successful in your... er... new profession, and I am delighted that you have returned to dear old Fawdon. You live at Dupont House now, I believe?' Laura leaned forward. 'And I did hear that you have finally completed all of the renovations, so much work to do in these old houses you know.'

Cynthia looked astonished, 'How did you know about the renovations, Miss Windle? I mean my house is at the other end of the village and you rarely come that way.'

'Merely by chance, my dear, or call it coincidence if you will. You see I happen to know Jim Brooks, the plumber, and I have had some problems with a tap washer in the kitchen lately. I can only think he must have mentioned it whilst working here... er, an avocado bathroom suite with bidet and shower, was it not?' Laura raised an eyebrow. 'That really must look splendid, and of course it is always best to get these alterations done before moving in.'

Cynthia nodded dumbly in response.

'But,' Laura went on, 'Can I assume that that was not the reason for your phone call and our meeting today?' She watched as Cynthia Roberts undid the straps on her briefcase and brought out a sheaf of papers.

'No, it's not, Miss Windle,' she replied. She looked down at the papers and sighed. 'I've come to see you because I need your help.'

Laura's gaze sharpened, she stared at the papers the woman was holding and resisted the urge to reach out for them. 'I will do whatever I can, if it is within my power,' she said quietly.

*

Cynthia looked up and saw the interest deepen in Miss Windle's eyes. Taking a deep breath she said. 'I can only start at the beginning, so here's how it happened. As you can imagine, since my husband's death I've put all of my energy into making a success of my career as a private investigator and I've been lucky…'

'The Lord works in mysterious ways,' Laura murmured.

'Yes,' Cynthia nodded in agreement, 'and business has been good, but,' she paused, 'and here the complications begin. Just after I had moved back into Fawdon, two separate clients came to see me in my Leeds office. These clients are not related or connected in any way. They are both hard-working people that have, until now, made a success of their lives. But because of mistakes they made in the past, they're being blackmailed.' Cynthia hesitated. 'I'm not even sure if it's the same blackmailer for both of my clients; there could be more than one. The important thing is that for reasons of either greed or envy, these two clients are being bled dry –'

'But,' Miss Windle interrupted sharply, 'surely you do not think that I..? You must remember…' she hesitated. 'Mrs Roberts, have I your permission to call you Cynthia?'

Cynthia nodded, 'Please do.'

'Well then Cynthia, you know why I had to apply some, shall we say leverage on you. It was for an excellent cause, and, I hate to have to remind you, but you had reneged on your promise to contribute –'

'Yes, yes, I do know that,' Cynthia protested hastily. 'This has nothing to do with that situation at all, and if you'll let me finish…'

'Of course.'

Cynthia said earnestly, 'The reason I have come to you for help on this is because you know just about everyone in the village.'

'This is true, to some extent. I have taught most of the villagers, some years ago of course, and if I have not taught them, I would know the parents or, 'Miss Windle smiled wryly, 'at my age, even the grandparents. But you must remember, my dear, that these days there are lots of new people moving into Fawdon. New businesses, new houses and so forth, so it will take some time for me to acquaint myself with them.'

'Would you know Martha McPherson?' Cynthia interrupted.

Miss Windle stopped in mid-sentence and stared at her. 'Mrs McPherson? The Proprietor of the Golden Rose Tea Shoppe? Of course I know her, a most respectable...' she broke off, 'surely she cannot be a victim?'

Cynthia looked at Miss Windle and saw that her face had turned quite pale, 'I'm afraid so,' she replied. 'I can't tell you the reason for the blackmail. As you must know, that is strictly confidential.'

'The name of the other client?' Miss Windle asked sharply.

'The owner of the Lorenzo Restaurant. Alfredo is his Christian name and he is very distressed,' Cynthia replied.

'So I can imagine.' Miss Windle said. 'Such a charming man, so helpful and so attentive, in spite of the fact that he is not English.'

Cynthia repressed a smile. 'Neither of the victims are, but that's not the reason for the blackmail.'

Miss Windle got to her feet, walked over to the window and looked out at the grey November skies. 'But,' she said thoughtfully, 'that might add to it.' She turned to look at her. 'Tell me as much as you think permissible, Cynthia.' She glanced at the papers that Cynthia still held. 'May I see those?'

'These are only copies of the letters the victims received,' Cynthia said as she got up and handed them to her. 'The originals are in a safe place.' She stood watching whilst Miss Windle read through the copies, before continuing. 'The common denominator is the post mark. These letters were posted in Fawdon. It seems likely that whoever is blackmailing these people either lives or has connections here in this village.'

Miss Windle pursed her lips and returned the letters. 'There are many that live here that might be tempted to be less than honest, but that they should be so greedy? I will help you, but I need time to think.'

Cynthia put the letters back in her briefcase and smiled gratefully. 'Somehow I knew you would.' She looked at her watch, then said, 'I've got to leave now. I've another appointment in ten minutes.'

'Not another 'victim?' Laura asked.

Cynthia said worriedly. 'I hope not, I'm hoping it might be on a different matter. I'm seeing Peter Greystone. I'm sure you know him? He's such a dear sweet man.'

'He is a fine watchmaker too,' Miss Windle fingered her wrist watch and smiled. 'He has repaired this and my kitchen clock on many occasions. Please give him my regards.' She walked with Cynthia through the hall, opened the door and said softly, 'Try not to worry too much, my dear. I will keep your secrets.'

Cynthia looked at her. 'Can I call on your help when I have more information? I'll be seeing Mrs McPherson later today.'

'Please do; anything at all.'

*

Laura watched Cynthia Roberts walk back up the path, get into her car and drive away. She closed the door gently, then leaned against it. When Cynthia had told her the names of the victims it was as if her friend Julia's last day on earth had come back to haunt her. She recalled the scene with Julia waving a sheet of paper in her face as if it were yesterday. She had only caught a brief look at the names on it, but at the top of the list had been the name Martha McPherson and below it had been Alfredo Lorenzo.

Clasping her hands together she hurried back into the living room and made straight for her writing desk. For a second she stared down at the desk, pondering. The notes of many incidents in her past were in the ledger, but as for that scrap of paper? Who had found it? She had thought it to be on the rubbish heap where it rightly belonged, but this was clearly not the case. This could not be coincidence, someone had found it. She knew there had been far more than those two names on that list and now it had fallen into the hands of individuals whose intentions were evil. She had to find it. This much was clear. She had to try to help Cynthia.... 'More than try,' she murmured. She knew that she, albeit inadvertently, was the root cause of it all.

Chapter Seven

Wednesday afternoon

Peter Greystone sat at his workbench and adjusted the spot light yet again. Taking off his glasses he rubbed at his eyes irritably then put the spectacles back on; it was no use, he'd have go back to the opticians, these new spectacles just weren't strong enough. Picking up a pair of tiny tweezers he continued his work, probing gently at the interior of the gentleman's wrist watch that he was working on. Finally he smiled in satisfaction and muttered, 'Just needed a bit of adjustment; that ought to do it.' Deftly he replaced the back of the watch, reset the hands and checked that it was working. Then he sat thoughtfully for a while, stroking its smooth gold casing. She should be here any minute, he thought. He looked with pride at the clocks and the watches that were on display all around him. It had taken him many years to establish his shop and his watch repairing business here in Fawdon. The main reason being that most of the villagers went into the city of Leeds to have their watches and jewellery repaired. But in time, the locals had come to him for their repairs – he was a working jeweller after all, not like some of the 'here today and gone tomorrow' blokes in the city who sent their repairs off to some backend workshop.

The villagers had discovered that his work was good and his charges reasonable. Gradually the retail side of his business had grown, with customers starting to buy small trinkets or costume jewellery when they came to collect their repairs and some of the good reliable watches that he stocked. As sales increased he'd thought about moving upmarket and stocking some of the really good jewellery, then he'd thought about the additional insurance he'd need to take out, to say nothing of the expensive security alarms that would be essential. There was of course another reason for not stocking more expensive goods. Peter's lips tightened as he reflected on that...

It was all so long ago, he'd thought it would be forgotten, he shook his head wearily, but no, it was not to be. Over two years ago he'd received a phone call from a woman asking if he was the same Peter Greystone who in the nineteen fifties had worked at a well-known jewellers in Hatton Garden. In all innocence he'd replied that he was, and that he'd done his apprenticeship there.

'Then you really are *the* Peter Greystone who was involved in the massive jewellery fraud case,' she'd said icily.

'Yes, but you see...' But that was enough. As he'd started to defend himself there'd been a click and the line went dead. He remembered staring at the phone in horror, thinking he'd got cut off and waiting for the woman to call back and give him a chance to explain, but she hadn't. He'd tried to think of a way of phoning her but then he'd realised she'd not given her name. He'd then assumed that she was some newspaper reporter. For weeks after that he'd worried, he'd checked the Evening Post every night and the local weekly paper for any mention of the fraud case, or his involvement with it, but there'd been nothing. After a few months he'd relaxed, it looked like it had just been a malicious phone call, nothing more. But now, after nearly two years, a letter had arrived.

He heard a car door slamming outside, and standing up, he walked towards the glass fronted shop door. Yes, across the road he could see the well-built figure of Mrs Roberts approaching. 'Maybe help is on the way,' he murmured hopefully as he went to welcome her

*

Cynthia smiled as she saw Peter Greystone; she looked at the small, slightly built man with his greyish blond hair and friendly grin and wondered why he'd asked her to call. He was such a pleasant family man with a wife and two daughters; she hoped he wasn't having marital problems. 'Sorry I'm a bit late, Mr Greystone,' she said as he ushered her into the shop. 'I got stuck down at the crossroads, the traffic lights have failed again.'

'Not to worry Mrs Roberts,' he said as he gestured towards a chair. 'I wasn't going anywhere. How's the grandmother clock doing now, is it working okay?'

'Yes, Gertie's doing fine.' Cynthia grinned at his puzzled expression. 'That's what Harry and I always called her, she's a bit temperamental, doesn't like moving house y'see.'

Mr Greystone smiled, 'Clocks are often like that, all it needed was a bit of cleaning. It's a fine piece of work though, must have cost a pretty penny?'

Cynthia laughed. 'It was one of my first big treats, bought it with my first months' pay.'

Mr Greystone raised an eyebrow. 'You must have had a good job then. What did you do?'

Whoops! Nearly slipped up there, Cynthia thought. She said. 'Er, this and that. Customer relations mainly,' she felt her face flush. 'Course I got lots of bonuses and tons of overtime too.' Clearing her throat she said very quickly. 'Now Mr Greystone, to business. What was it you wanted to talk to me about?'

He went back round the counter then said. 'Before we start, how about a nice cup of tea?'

'Lovely, yes please.' Cynthia watched as he disappeared into the back room and called, 'Milk but no sugar and no biscuits, thanks.' She touched her thighs; the last thing she needed was more flab on her hips. Cynthia looked around at the glass cabinets that encircled her and felt tempted at the selection of so many pretty necklaces and bracelets that were displayed there. How nice to be surrounded by such lovely things when you are working, she thought, but then again if I worked here the constant ticking of all the clocks on the walls would take some getting used to.

'Here we are then.' Mr Greystone said as he returned and placed the tea tray on the counter. 'You be Mother... that should warm us up.'

He watched whilst she poured out the hot tea and they drank it together. When they'd finished he went to his workbench and opened the drawer. 'Now for the reason I phoned you,' he said, 'but first, Mrs Roberts, can you assure me that this conversation remains strictly confidential?'

'Of course it will be, but you do know that if you've committed any crime, I'm bound by law to report it to the police.' Cynthia replied.

'Well yes, I knew that, but then the reason I called you, was because I wanted to show you this.' He returned to the counter and handed her a small white envelope, then he sat down and waited until she finished reading the contents.

After a few minutes Cynthia put down the letter, looked at him and asked, 'Is this true?'

'Let me tell you what happened.' He rubbed at his forehead wearily. 'It was all so long ago. You see, back in the Fifties, my parents, having noticed I was good at making and repairing fragile things, decided to get me an apprenticeship at this large jewellers in London. I was thrilled to bits – I loved the idea of working with such fine jewels and rare metals. I was there for four years until I knew about most things in the jewellery business, from the manufacturing side at least.' He gave a tired smile. 'Let's say, I thought I did, but then you know what lads in their early twenties are like. Everything was fine, I was well paid, I'd met

Helen, the love of my life, and we were saving to get married and build a home together.'

Then one day one of my bosses came to me... did I mention that we did lots of valuations? Well this boss was in charge of that section of the business. He chatted about this and that, told me how well I was doing, even hinted at a pay rise. Then he mentioned a necklace that we had in for a repair and valuation, sapphires and platinum it was; a superb piece of work. He said that somehow the hallmark on the clasp had got damaged and could I, just as a favour, put the correct hallmark back on it. Yes, I said, I could and I did, but then soon after that, as weeks passed, two or three pieces of jewellery arrived on my workbench, all with some kind of damage. I became suspicious; I began to examine the jewels more thoroughly and whilst repairing the gold claws that were warped in one diamond necklace, I noticed that some of the stones seemed a bit more sparkly than the others. I looked at them again. This time very closely. I discovered to my horror that two of the stones in the necklace were cubic zirconias. I couldn't believe what I was seeing. I was holding a beautiful old necklace from a long standing customer. I knew it came in every year for cleaning and small repairs and that all of the stones were diamonds. Until now. What was happening? I thought this through and I was terrified. Someone was substituting the jewels and it wasn't me. I knew I had to do something, but didn't know who to talk to. One thing was certain. If I spoke to the wrong person, I'd lose my job.'

Peter Greystone sighed. 'The truth was, Mrs Roberts, I was scared witless about having to report this to my boss. But, after a week of sleepless nights I finally plucked up the courage and made an appointment for the next day to see the man at the top, even if it would cost me my job.

The following morning I arrived at the store only to find the entrance surrounded by newspaper reporters. I knew I was too late. I ran back the way I came, and as I reached the corner of the road I passed a newspaper seller. On the placard in front of him was the headline, "London Jewellers accused of massive fraud."'

Cynthia leaned forward. 'What happened then?'

'Nothing for a while, I stayed in my flat, too scared to go out. Then two days later the police arrived and asked me to accompany them to the police station.' He sighed, 'I knew it was all over. I got sent down of course, they charged me with 'conspiracy to fraud,' even though I'd been following the instructions of one of my bosses.' I should have gone with my gut feeling and reported what I'd found straight away, but I was too scared... Anyway I did my time and when I came out we moved north back up to Yorkshire. I knew that with my record, no jeweller would employ me even though I'd served my punishment. So, because the jewellery business was all I knew, I decided to become self-employed. I found this little shop.' He paused, 'Did you know it used to be a cobbler's shop?'

Cynthia shook her head. 'But then we only lived here for five years,' she said.

'Well some instinct told me this little shop was right. I worked long and hard, charging next to nothing for my repairs until I earned a comfortable living... and now this.'

'Mr Greystone, you've nothing to fear.'

He picked up the letter then looked at her wearily. 'Mrs Roberts, I ask you honestly, would you bring your jewellery to me for repair if you knew I'd done time for jewellery fraud?' He saw her hesitate then said flatly. 'Mud sticks; if this becomes public I'll be in the dole queue within a month.'

'How did this woman caller realise it could be you? How did she make the connection?' Cynthia asked.

'I've thought about this and the only thing that could have caught her attention was an article in the paper nearly three years ago. It mentioned this well-known London jewellers opening a new branch in Leeds. In it they referred to the famous fraud case of the Fifties, they also gave the names of the people involved in the fraud. My name was amongst them. It was only a short article and I'd hoped people wouldn't notice.'

'But *she* sure did.'

Mr Greystone looked across at her and lifted his hands in exasperation 'What are the odds on that?'

Cynthia sighed. 'There's an old saying, "If it can go wrong, it will do." But what puzzles me is, why this silence? Why is there this gap since the woman called you before you received this letter?'

She said cautiously, 'I take it this is the only letter you've received?'

He looked down at the letter then began to place it back in its envelope. 'Yes, I got it a few days ago. It came through the post with the rest of the mail. A hundred pounds is a hell of a lot of money, my first impulse was to tear it up, but then I thought...'

'So you've not made the payment?'

'No. I decided to phone you.' He pulled out the letter again and read its contents out loud.

'The money is to be placed at the entrance to Mallins Mill next Saturday night at 7.30. Don't be late or else.'

Cynthia said earnestly, 'Mr Greystone, I've got to tell you that this is blackmail. You are well within your rights to take this to the police.'

'No, no, no! I'll not do that. The last thing I need is more publicity and should this come out...'

'What do you want me to do?'

He said grimly. 'Get this thieving villain and find some way of silencing him.'

Chapter Eight

Wednesday
4pm

Cynthia sat in her car outside Martha's Golden Rose Tea Shoppe and thought about Peter Greystone and Martha McPherson. Both were being blackmailed but as Martha had to pay up on Friday, Cynthia had to concentrate on her first. She thought about Martha's case. Martha had told her that this was all because of a dangerous driving accident she'd had some years ago. The victim had not died but had been seriously injured. Then, with some reluctance, she'd told Cynthia that although she'd taken the rap for that charge it had been her husband who'd been driving and he'd *persuaded her* to tell the court that she'd been the driver.

Cynthia felt puzzled by this; she wondered why Martha's husband would make her give false evidence. She'd tried to probe further, but Martha had seemed reluctant to discuss the matter further. She'd stated flatly that they were now divorced and then quickly changed the subject. Cynthia felt uneasy at this; some instinct told her she wasn't hearing the whole truth.

With a sigh, Cynthia switched on the ignition and drove off towards Leeds. Ten minutes later she was easing her way through the heavy traffic in Kirkstall Road. She scowled, her headache was increasing by the second and she knew the cause of that was that she'd not had lunch. She'd felt hungry earlier but she'd been reluctant to fill up on biscuits and crisps. She sighed, she was doomed to be one of those women who had to constantly watch their weight.

A car horn blared loudly and Cynthia started, 'watch it girl,' she told herself, otherwise you're not going to reach your office in one piece. She checked the time on the dashboard clock; 4.45 and the rush hour had already started. She stared gloomily at the red brake lights in front of her and knew it would be like this, nose to tail, until they reached the city centre, there was no quick way of getting anywhere fast at this hour of the day.

Cynthia's thoughts drifted back over the day's events and her headache increased. These cases of blackmail were almost epidemic – two, possibly three blackmail clients in one village and all of them at roughly the same time, what on earth was going on?

She thought again about the latest letter Martha McPherson had handed to her. Yet another ultimatum for more cash, this time on Friday night at 7pm. And, so Mrs McPherson had told her, this was the third demand for yet a further 100 pounds. Cynthia had clicked her tongue as she heard that, but Martha had said she'd been so terrified when she'd received the first letter that she'd paid the money immediately and that it was only after she'd paid again that she'd summoned up the courage to contact her. Cynthia pondered, she could understand why people allowed themselves to be blackmailed; she knew from personal experience that everyone has secrets. Even today the very idea of someone identifying her as a former call girl sent a shiver down her spine. Of course that blackmailing situation had been resolved now, and her Harry was gone, so he couldn't be hurt anymore. Cynthia bit on her lip as she eased the car into its parking space. Now she wouldn't much care if details of her former life did come out, although it could affect her business. She got out of the car, walked up to her office and smiled whimsically as she thought that through. Opening the door she picked up the mail from the mat. Who knows, it could even bring in additional customers.

She went to her desk, sat down and began to open the letters. She pulled a face, most of them were bills; she would deal with them later. She pushed them back into her 'in' tray then checked her appointments book. Her spirits lifted as she read the name and the venue of her next possible contract. Distant memories of this place returned and she smiled in recollection. This was one occasion where she would happily mix business with pleasure.

Chapter Nine

Thursday evening
6.45pm

Alfredo Lorenzo stood in his restaurant and fiddled nervously with the small flower vase on one of the tables. The red spray carnations were fine and fresh, but the ferns that encircled them were looking tired. He lifted them out, saw that the stems were broken, snipped at them quickly with his finger nails and returned them to the vase. Having done this he looked around his domain, his eyes scanning the tables, checking for any marks on the cloths or signs of disarray. Seeing that all was well he began to pace the floor, every so often looking anxiously at the restaurant door. He tried not to look at his watch, his appointment was for 7pm and there was no logical reason why Cynthia Roberts should arrive early. As for tonight's reservations, his first customers weren't due to arrive until 8.pm which should allow him plenty of time to discuss his problem.

He felt in his jacket pocket and fingered the envelopes uneasily. How could anyone have found out about...? How did they know what his real name was?

His gaze strayed yet again towards the restaurant entrance. What was he to tell Cynthia?

He still found it difficult to realise that she was now a private investigator. The Cynthia Roberts and her husband, Harry, that he'd known, had been regular customers at his establishment, but that had been over two years ago. He'd heard about Harry's death of course and, more recently, about Cynthia establishing her own business as a P.I. and returning to live in Fawdon. Now as he waited for her arrival he wondered whether he'd done the right thing in making an appointment to see her. But one thing was certain, he sure needed help.

His restlessness increased. He strode to the front of the restaurant, opened the door, and on the pretence of checking the menu at the entrance, peered down the High Street hopefully.

He heard the tapping of her heels on the pavement seconds before she called out, 'Hello, Alfredo! How are you?'

Surprised he spun round to face her. She was just as glamorous as he'd remembered, with her auburn curls and pretty face. Slim she was not; she was what he would call womanly. 'Cynthia!' he said. 'I was looking... I thought you would have come here from the other end of the street?'

'Sorry if I'm a bit early but I'd a letter to post first,' she smiled. She stared up at him thoughtfully, then touched his arm. 'So, really, how are you?'

He looked down at her. 'Quite well, I would say. But come, let's go inside.' He guided her through the doors and seated her at a table at the rear of the restaurant. 'Firstly, a glass of wine,

Signora?' He bowed and touched his temple as if remembering. 'As I recall, a glass of Chianti... a large one?' He raised an eyebrow.

'Of course,' Cynthia laughed. 'Seeing as I only need to walk home from here.'

He brought the bottle of wine and glasses to the table, poured a large glass for Cynthia and a little more than a sip full for himself.

'As for food, I would recommend...'

'No food just yet, Alfredo.' Cynthia interrupted. 'You called me here on business so let's deal with your problem first, then I can enjoy my meal later.'

'As you wish.' For a moment Alfredo shifted uneasily in his chair then brought the two offending envelopes from his pocket, put them on the table and placed his hand firmly over them.

Cynthia stared at them. 'Aren't you going to show me?'

Alfredo hesitated, 'I will show you the letters but there are many other things I need to tell you first... if you will listen?'

Cynthia nodded in agreement.

'To begin, a little of my family history,' Alfredo said. 'Although I was born in Sheffield I spent many years as a boy living in Naples with my father and my stepmother, Sophia. I grew up learning the Italian language and, as my stepmother was an excellent cook, loving the Italian food.' He sighed. 'I was only a teenager when Sophia died and my dad and I returned to England. It was hard for both of us, I had no work experience but I was lucky enough to get work as a trainee chef in an Italian restaurant in Sheffield.'

He leaned forward confidingly. 'There I was known by my real English name, Alfred Lawrence.'

Cynthia giggled. 'Alfred Lawrence equals Alfredo Lorenzo, it's very logical, I really should have guessed. That's why you named this restaurant, 'Lorenzo's.'

He nodded, 'I'll let you into another secret, I'm also known to my close friends in Sheffield as 'Alfie,' but I digress. Life was good to me in Sheffield. I worked hard, saved and eventually got my own place. I called it, 'Napoli,' in memory of my childhood and my stepmother. Time passed, the business was successful; I married. Then my luck began to change. My wife, Anne, decided she wanted children.' Alfredo paused and stared hard at Cynthia, 'I must tell you, I am not a family man. All I wanted was a profitable business. Perhaps you will understand me better if I tell you that as a boy in Naples, I had seen far too much poverty.'

Cynthia reached across the table and touched his hand. 'I understand perfectly, Alfredo,' she said quietly. 'You don't have to justify yourself to me or to anyone else for that matter.'

He sighed in relief, 'For me, money is very important. And so Anne left me, she found another love and they now have a family.' His fingers smoothed the tablecloth, 'And I worked harder than ever. The business boomed, yet I wanted more.' He looked across at Cynthia, 'I should tell you there are many ways of making money in the food business if you cut corners.'

'I might have known. And you…'

'Began to take risks. Third quality meat, poor vegetables and still my business prospered. Until one day I bought some mushrooms – they looked okay, but they were sold at a ridiculous price…'

'Mushrooms! Oh Alfredo,' Cynthia blurted, 'even I know about the dangers of mushrooms.'

'Of course I knew it was risky but the thing was, those first baskets of mushrooms were fine, no problem at all.'

'They'd be what is known as 'bait,'' Cynthia muttered.

'Next time I doubled the order and then…' Alfredo broke off and held his head in his hands, 'all hell exploded upon me! Dozens of cases of food poisoning, all leading back to my place. My restaurant became infamous! It made the front page in the local paper.' He sat upright and looked straight at her. 'I did all I could, I settled most of the cases out of court with my own money, but there was one elderly couple, regular customers, who were badly affected. They were gravely ill in hospital for a long time. I was very fond of them, I tried my best to help them, but they never forgave me.' He sighed again, 'I had to close. With the money I had left I came here and built up this place.'

Cynthia gestured at the letters. 'So what's all this about?'

Alfredo picked up one envelope, withdrew the sheet of paper and read out loud.

'I know about you, Alfred Lawrence, you poisoner. You should be in hell where you belong. If you want me to remain silent put £100 in an envelope and leave it in the graveyard at Sam Frystone's tombstone under the flower vase on Sunday 17th December.'

'Why that particular date?' Cynthia interrupted. She nearly blurted out that her other clients both had received demands for this week, but on second thoughts, she decided to stay silent about that.

Alfredo shrugged his shoulders and looked at her in frustration. 'I don't know. Maybe he is busy collecting money elsewhere on other days.'

Cynthia had to suppress a grin as the thoughts of a blackmailer being so busy he had to work overtime flashed through her mind. Be serious, she told herself, the writer of this letter is a greedy and cruel person. She cleared her throat and looked at Alfredo. 'H'mm,' she said. 'May I see?' He handed her the letter. It was in the same style as the other letters which Peter Greystone and Martha Mcpherson had received. Same cheap paper, black ink script and block capitals. She read through it again; only this time, whoever wrote this was using more words and gaining confidence.

'May I see the envelope. Alfredo?'

'It arrived at the beginning of the week.' He said as he gave it to her. 'It came by post along with the rest of the mail.'

Cynthia nodded, as she expected it was a white envelope similar to the ones her other clients had received and, importantly, it had the Fawdon postmark. So, she thought, whoever is sending this may not live in Fawdon, but they certainly know someone who does. She looked at him. 'Have you contacted the police about this?'

Alfredo said wearily. 'Cynthia, I do not want to go down that road again. As I told you, I did wrong. But I did all I could to put things right. And now this. It is to me as if they are opening an old wound that I thought was healed.'

'Alfredo,' Cynthia said gently, 'This is a threatening letter. All this person really wants is your money. You have paid the price. Are you prepared to pay again?

'No!' Alfredo slammed his hands down hard on the table, 'Never!'

'Right then, Cynthia said, 'what we'll do is…'

'Cynthia!' He waved the second envelope in front of her, 'you've not seen this.'

She took it from him, opened the envelope and withdrew a yellowed square of newsprint. Emblazoned on it was the photo of the 'Napoli,' restaurant. Across the restaurant window was a large 'Closed' poster, and below the picture, an article giving details of the poisoning cases. At the bottom of the newsprint were the printed words

'In case you think I don't have proof.'

Cynthia sighed. 'He's telling you he means business.'

'But,' protested Alfredo, 'it is *this business* that is at stake, what will happen if this becomes public knowledge? In a village like this. I will be ruined!'

'Do you want me to do something about this?'

'Of course, but,' he turned and looked nervously towards the kitchen. 'There is another problem.' He got up and beckoned, 'Come with me.' He strode into the kitchen area where the back door of the restaurant was situated. Cynthia followed him and watched as he went to the door, bent down and picked up a plastic bag with a dustpan inside it. He opened the bag and showed her the contents of the dustpan, 'These I found this morning.'

Cynthia peered at them. They looked like pepper corns, but Cynthia knew different. She stared up at him. 'Alfredo, these are mouse droppings.'

He drew himself up to his full six feet and said, 'No! This cannot be. This restaurant does not and never has had mice.'

Suspicion dawned in Cynthia's mind – putting mice droppings in someone's kitchen, was hardly the modus operandi of a blackmailer who was already sending letters to victims in this village. So then..?

'Why is this happening to me?' Alfredo's voice broke in on her thoughts.

'For heaven's sake get rid of that,' she gestured at the contents of the dustpan, 'before your customers come in.' She walked back to her table, sat down and took a thoughtful sip from her wine.

After a minute Alfredo followed and sat down opposite her again. 'So then, what am I to do?'

'Alfredo, the first question that springs to mind is how did the blackmailer find out about this poisoning case?'

'I wish I knew; I've racked my brains trying to think of anyone that I might have mentioned this to. The only thing I can think of was... but that was oh so long ago, almost three years. Some old friends had come to visit me on my birthday. We had food and wine in here to celebrate, where else? We got talking about the old days in Sheffield. Someone mentioned the poison case; the wine was flowing, maybe they were a bit loud. I did not worry; I thought no one had heard him. There was only a group of old ladies from the Women's Institute having dinner that night, and they all seemed to be too busy gossiping.'

At the mention of 'old ladies from the Women's Institute,' a vision of Laura Windle shot into Cynthia's mind; she took a large gulp from her wine and dismissed the thought immediately. But two years? Almost three years? Cynthia thought. 'Why does that number of years keep re-occurring in these cases? There must be some connection.

'Alfredo,' she said, 'if you give me permission I'll do what I can to trace this blackmailer and try to put things right.' She hesitated and her glance strayed again towards the kitchen. 'But as for the mouse droppings? I hate to say this, but it seems to me that more than one person has taken a distinct dislike to you.'

Chapter Ten

An hour later, Cynthia, having enjoyed a delicious Pollo Cocciatora, and determinedly resisted the temptation of a dessert, came out of 'Lorenzo's' and strolled along the High Street towards her home. She felt contented and a little drowsy and she knew this was due to the food and wine. Already she was beginning to feel a little bit of regret; she knew she would have to return to a strict diet for at least a week so that tonight's excesses didn't go straight to her hips.

She thought about Alfredo – such an attractive man with his expressive brown eyes, his dark wavy hair and his natural charm. He would be quite a catch for some woman, as long as they were as dedicated as he was to being in business and making money. But now he was her client and she would do all she could to help him. She thought again about the arrangements they had planned. She would check out the mentioned gravestone in the graveyard next week. Meanwhile as her other two clients had pick up places this week, they had to have priority. She would deal with Martha McPherson's arranged rendezvous first.

Tomorrow night Martha McPherson had her pick up point at the bowling green shed. Then on Saturday there was Peter's nocturnal appointment at Mallins Mill. As for Alfredo's meeting at the

Graveyard, for reasons best known to the blackmailer, it was to be on the Sunday mentioned in the letter. That at least would give her some breathing space. Cynthia took a deep breath as she thought of all the work she would have to do. In her line of business it was all or nothing and this looked like it was going to be one hectic week.

As she passed the florist's lighted window, she paused to look at the beautiful display; it did her heart good to see something as lovely as flowers when her work meant dealing with something as ugly as blackmail. She thought back to those times in her youth when she'd received beautiful flowers and corsages from her 'grateful clients,' and she smiled cynically, then the flowers were the only innocent part of those transactions. These days she was grateful when the cheques she received in payment for her work didn't bounce.

She stood for a moment admiring the colours of the blooms and her thoughts turned to her own weed-covered back garden; she really should do something about that. Perhaps Mr Mitchell might know of a gardener?

She would have to find the time to call in on Mr Mitchell and ask his advice. With that thought in her mind she strolled on towards her cottage.

Chapter Eleven

Friday morning
8.30am

Simon had just finished sweeping the pavement in front of his shop and was about to put the buckets of mixed bunches and chrysanthemums outside, when a white van pulled up in front of the empty premises across the road. He leaned on his broom and watched as the driver, a thin man with sleek black hair got out, nodded briefly at him, then hurried round to the side door of the shop.

Simon's interest deepened, he swept the pavement a bit more and hung around in the hope that he would see some of the goods that the driver might bring out of the van. But he was to be disappointed. The man came back, climbed into the van then reversed in front of the garage next to the shop's side door. The van was now parked so that no one could see what was inside it.

Simon scowled, marched back into his own emporium and slammed the door. Was it his imagination or was the new tenant being intentionally secretive? The man certainly wasn't friendly, he could have at least managed a 'good morning.' That would have given Simon the excuse to stroll across the road, offer the man a mug of tea and then get the chance to have a quick once over of the stock.

Simon picked up the buckets of flowers and taking them outside, stood staring across the road at the empty shop. He felt the curiosity grow in him. Something was not right. The new tenant, if that was the man he'd just seen, was unfriendly. That in itself was unusual in this village, people here were very sociable. He remembered the days, about six years ago now, when old Jimmy Finch used to have that shop. It was an ironmongers back then and there were always customers wandering in and out. Old Jimmy had sold just about everything you could think of in the hardware line – pots, pans, spades, chicken wire, even pet food. But that was before the coming of the big supermarkets that also sold everything, but at a much lower price.

When Jimmy retired he'd tried to sell the business, but there'd been no takers, so he'd just locked up, leaving the shop empty, and gone to live in Cornwall.

If only, Simon thought, he could find out what the new tenant was going to sell? He could not rely on rumours. It was November and he wondered whether the man would be of the 'pile 'em high and sell 'em cheap' brigade that opened in December, selling cheap Christmas sundries and then upping sticks by early February.

A horrible thought came into his mind. What if the man were to sell Christmas Trees and Christmas wreaths? That could mean a cut price war. He'd already placed his order for several dozen of each of these from a local grower and such things were perishable stock. His resolve deepened, it was no use, he had to find out what was on those premises. He heard the vehicle start up and watched as the white van drove off. He didn't stay long, so he can't have unloaded much. Simon looked along the High Street, the other shops were opening up and the young mothers with their kiddies were already out and about and on their way to school. Now was not the time to go 'investigating.' Best go find his big torch and some other tools that prove useful and wait until tonight. Old Jimmy's locks would still be on the doors, so they'd be a bit rusty by now; it shouldn't take much effort to bust them open and have a little scout round.

Chapter Twelve

Claire Forbes walked over to the window, straightened her newly draped curtains and looked out at the small overgrown garden in disgust. She didn't know much about gardens, but even she knew that this bit of land in front of her house needed a good seeing to. She would have to find someone to cement over it and tidy it up a bit. Maybe put some of those stone Grecian urn things in each corner, with some of those pink geraniums perhaps? Yeah, that'd be alright, and then she wouldn't need to bother about it anymore.

She leaned up against the window and peered along the street; what a weird little village Fawdon was, only one High Street, a bit like out of a nursery rhyme with a few shops spotted along it. A butcher and a baker, but no bloody candlestick maker. Claire grinned at that thought, then her lips tightened. Still no ruddy hairdresser either, let alone a nice dress shop. She'd have to go into Leeds for that. Still, she consoled herself with the fact that she'd not be here for long.

She looked around at the front room with its high ceiling, ornate cornice and old fashioned coal fireplace, and scowled. She'd got the gas man coming tomorrow to see to that fireplace. She was certainly not going to be on her knees fiddling around with firelighters when perfectly good gas fires were available. Another problem was what was she to do with the coal that was in the cellar, she'd have to find a buyer for that somehow. As she thought about that she shivered, for some reason this room still felt cold even though she'd put a portable electric heater in here and it was going full blast.

She crossed the hall and wandered into the kitchen. She had no right to be ungrateful though – this Victorian semi-detached had been an unexpected gift from her big sister, and it had come at a time when she'd been desperate. What a change from her cramped bed-sit in Sheffield, where every week she'd had to struggle to scrape the rent money together. But now? She rubbed her hands together excitedly as she looked around. Now she was a property owner, a woman with *collateral* and soon she'd make very sure this house fetched a good price. That is, when she was ready to go.

She filled the kettle, placed it on the old fashioned gas hob and stared down at it in bewilderment for a few seconds, before remembering that she needed to light the damned thing. Swearing loudly she turned the gas off, rushed to get her handbag, found her lighter and lit the gas. 'What a bloody performance,' she grumbled, 'all for the sake of a cup of tea.'

Having made her drink, she sat down at the kitchen table, lit a cigarette and pondered. She thought about the letter and the birthday card and the other stuff she'd received from her snobby big sister two years ago, and how her first reaction was that this was spitefulness from a lonely old woman and she'd wanted to just chuck it away. She'd shown Julia's letter to all of her friends and they'd laughed about it, but then... Then, only a few weeks later came the awful phone call and the news that her sister had died in a tragic accident. Claire still felt a twinge of guilt when she remembered that day. After all, they were sisters and if only Julia hadn't been so critical of everything that she did... perhaps then they could have got along better? It was no use. She was what she was and Julia should have accepted it. Claire sat up straight and looked around... but who would have thought that Julia would leave her this house in her will? This windfall couldn't have come at a better time. So here she was and she was determined to enjoy her new lifestyle. She would miss some of her friends though, but not all of them.

Claire grinned as she thought about that and she thought about Lennie. Now he was special. True he was a bit on the scrawny side for her taste, but he was ever so elegant in the way that he dressed and being tall, he carried his clothes well. He always had plenty of cash on him and he had a lovely big car; it was some kind of foreign make. She giggled in reminiscence, and it was ever so comfortable when they had a cuddle. Lennie was brainy too; one of life's entrepreneurs, you could say. Always had his fingers in lots of pies, and he knew all that there was to know about business deals and such. She missed him already but it wouldn't be for long. Two weeks ago, he'd phoned her to say he'd soon be moving into

Fawden, as he'd rented a little business there. "Should turn out to be a right little gold mine," he'd said. Claire smiled at this comforting thought. It looked like he was the one great love of her life. He'd gone to so much trouble just to be near her. She smiled in contentment; she'd always had plenty of male friends, and these days even more admirers. But as for Lennie? Well he was different, always full of big ideas.

Claire got up, walked to the window, looked down the road again and saw the postman approaching. After moving to Fawdon she'd decided it might be a good idea to get a job. She'd already applied for several in Leeds. She wanted something on a part time basis, maybe something in sales, or even some filing work. The last things she wanted was to be rattling around in this old place all day. The bit of extra money would be useful, although if things worked out well, she doubted if she would need it.... The click of the front gate disturbed her chain of thought and she jumped up to answer the door. With any luck there'd be some letters with replies in answer to her job applications.

Chapter Thirteen

Friday evening

Cynthia looked at the clock, clicked her tongue and hurried upstairs to get changed. She'd better get ready.

She went into the bedroom, kicked off her high heels, undressed, then pulled on some black slacks and went to rummage in the bottom of her wardrobe until she found the shoes she needed. Sitting down on the bed she put them on and as she did, wondered just how fast she'd be able to run tonight if push came to shove. Not very fast, she supposed, it had been many years since she'd done any running. She made a mental note to seek out some keep fit evening classes, and this time to try really hard to attend them. She gave a deep sigh, providing of course that business allowed.

Standing up she glanced in the mirror, then got a black sweater out of a drawer and put it on. She returned to the mirror and regarded her reflection with a critical eye. 'Still look like an oversized black pudding,' she grumbled. That remark took her back to the time a few years ago when she'd dressed up for her Harry. She smiled whimsically, although then her outfit and her motive had been more... seductive. She remembered how in an effort to get Harry out of his sombre mood she had dressed up, using her biker helmet, a face mask, fishnet tights and a whip, in an effort to seduce him. The result had been a disaster. It had brought on Harry's first heart attack. Then what had been intended as a joke and a bit of fun had turned into a frightening and life changing situation.

For a moment Cynthia stared thoughtfully into the mirror, she still felt guilt and a sense of horror when she thought about that night, but she hadn't known that Harry was on medication for his heart. 'He should have told me,' she muttered angrily. She stared again into the mirror, how she wished she could turn time back to those happier days. After a couple of seconds she shrugged her shoulders.

'Well you can't,' she told herself. Life goes on and she had a living to earn. Then she pulled a face at her reflection and said, 'Come on woman, let's get on with the job,' and went downstairs.

*

5.50pm

Cynthia walked over to the window and looked out into the night. It was almost six o'clock. Most of the shops would be closed and with any luck she'd be able to walk unnoticed along the High Street until she reached the Bowling Green on White Hart Close. She went into the hall and put on her black anorak, pulling the hood up so that it covered her distinctive, auburn curls.

'There,' she thought, 'not many of the Fawdoners will recognise me now.'

Closing the front door behind her she set off towards the High Street. The night was cold and she shivered, it would have been much easier to have driven, but she knew that there were many details that she simply wouldn't notice when driving a car. As she walked along, she felt in her coat pocket for the crumpled notes she had taken earlier in the day. She'd spent a good hour over at the Central Library in Leeds looking through the micro fiches of the national papers from eight years ago. It had taken her quite a while but eventually she'd found Martha McPherson's case. After checking up on what her client had told her, she knew it was all as she'd said, only Cynthia still had this feeling that Martha was holding something back. How had her husband *persuaded* her? What kind of leverage had he used? She felt frustrated; if she was to do her job properly she needed to know all the facts. It seemed that Martha was the perfect victim for any kind of blackmailer, for she had let fear control her entire life.

A car raced past at high speed with its engine roaring and Cynthia jumped, she looked around and her thoughts returned to the job in hand. She turned off the High Street and walked along the short cul-de-sac of White Hart Close towards the bowling green. She would need to look at the area carefully and suss out any convenient hiding places. Having reached the small wrought iron gate at the entrance, she winced at its stubbornly loud creak when she eased her way through and walked towards the hut door. Fishing her torch from her pocket, she allowed the light from it to fall on the lock. Taking hold of the handle, she tried the door, and nodded in satisfaction to find it locked – no hiding place there. She turned and walked along the path bordering the green. She began to feel uneasy, lots of thick scrubs and bushes, to say nothing of the huge old oak tree in the far corner. You could hide an army behind that trunk. She went up to the tree and walked round it, yes it certainly was an excellent place to hide. There must be something she could do that would tell her if someone should decide to conceal themselves there. She looked around and breaking some branches from the nearby bushes, scattered them on the ground around the tree. The twigs were dry and brittle, should anyone choose to hide there at least she'd be able to hear them.

She walked back to the bowling green hut and stood searching for a suitable observation post for herself. It would have to be somewhere close to the hut door so she could keep an eye on the bag. But now she'd have to get her car, collect Martha and park in the High Street, leaving Martha in the car until it was time. Then at 6.55pm, Martha would go to the hut and put the bag containing the money near the hut door.

Of course the bag wouldn't contain money; all it would hold were some useless bits of paper. Cynthia was not prepared to allow some evil sod to get away with a hundred pounds of someone else's hard earned cash. She hurried back home, got the car out from the garage and went to collect Martha.

*

6.55pm

The moon was nearly full now, a cold wind had started up and from the back of a large rhododendron bush Cynthia shivered. She shone her torch down on to her watch and felt her pulse quicken. Everything was in place as she looked towards the wrought iron gate at the entrance of the bowling-green and listened for any sounds of someone approaching. She was almost sure they would need to come in that way as the green was completely surrounded by high wooden fencing. But what if they were already here? What if they'd nipped in to the bowling green when she'd gone to collect Martha? Cynthia looked at the other bushes and eyed the old oak tree suspiciously. Holding her breath, she strained her ears to listen. All was still, not the slightest sound, only a solitary mouse, on a mission of its own, scurried silently across the path in front of her.

On seeing it Cynthia bit back the need to cry out and swallowed hard. Screaming at mice was for little girls, she was far too professional for that. She checked her watch again, two minutes to seven – Martha was due any minute now. She'd already briefed her on what she had to do. Cynthia just hoped she would get it right and place the bag at the door as the blackmailer had demanded. When she'd left Martha in the car on the High Street she'd seemed close to tears and more than ever Cynthia was convinced there was something that Martha was not telling her. She only hoped that she wouldn't try to confront the blackmailer, or, even worse, get half way to the meeting point then panic and turn around.

The sound of footsteps and the creaking of the Iron Gate brought Cynthia back to the present. Sure enough it was Martha coming towards her. She watched as the woman walked past her and up to the hut door. Martha looked around nervously for a second, then dropped the bag and hurried back to the exit as fast as her legs would carry her.

For a moment Cynthia allowed herself to relax as she watched the departing figure go through the gate and hurry off in the direction of the High Street. Good girl, she thought, no fuss, no panic, Martha had done exactly as she'd been told. At least that part of the job was done, now all she could do was wait and see what happens...

Ten minutes passed and the wind increased. Cynthia, in spite of her warm clothing, was starting to feel cold. Her hands felt numb and she rubbed her fingers together in an effort to generate some heat. Perhaps she'd been spotted; perhaps the blackmailer had already been there, seen her and scarpered. She'd give it another five minutes and then call it a night, before she froze to death.

There! What was that? A sort of scraping squeaking sound, then nothing. She listened intently... it seemed to be coming from the fencing behind the oak tree. Then, unmistakeably she heard it... the sound of twigs snapping. She held her breath. As she waited, a quote from her school days slipped into her mind, "By the pricking of my thumbs, something wicked this way comes." Sure enough a small, darkly clad, hooded figure was hurrying towards the bowling hut.

Cynthia's first instinct was to run to it and give it a good shaking, but she remembered her training and waited. She watched impatiently as the person bent down, picked up the bag, then with astonishing speed raced to the exit and vaulted clean over the Iron Gate.

Cynthia gasped! She gaped after the fleeing figure then set of after it. 'Run woman, run,' she told herself urgently 'don't you dare let him escape.' She raced out of the bowling green and up the High Street, praying with all her might that she'd catch him. She'd almost given up when she saw the figure look over his shoulder and stumble. Her luck was in! In one final spurt she reached him and grabbed frantically at the hood. The figure pulled away, then gasped.

'Don't hit me missus! I was only doing what he said.'

Cynthia stared uncomprehendingly at the curly headed girl who was facing her... This was surely not what "something wicked" looked like.

'What? Where? Who? 'She stammered.

'That mister,' the girl pointed up the street, 'in the car up at the cross roads,' She looked up at Cynthia pleadingly, 'Please let me go missus, he said he'd give me a quid if I'd fetch this bag, and if I don't he says he'll find me and I'll get a belting.'

Cynthia pushed back her anorak hood and stared down at the little girl; she couldn't be more than nine or ten years old. What was she to do? If she took the bag off her then the man would know someone was on to him.

'Do you know this man?'

'Nah,' said the little girl, 'but he did say he'd give me a quid.' She stared up at her with innocent eyes, then said earnestly, 'I know he will, 'cause he promised.'

Cynthia felt saddened. She needed to know who this man was. The thing to do was follow the girl. Reluctantly she said, 'Go on then, I'll let you go, but don't run so fast this time, give him the bag, but not a word about seeing me.'

The girl grinned in relief, 'I'm not daft, missus.' And she sprinted off up the street towards the crossroads.

After her! Cynthia thought and, keeping a safe distance from the girl, she followed. She had nearly reached the top of the street when she saw the girl turn right on to the crossroads. Panic gripped Cynthia, now the girl was out of sight; she must run faster. With all of her strength she raced up the street and turned on to the crossroads. But too late, she was just in time to see a large dark car pull sharply away from the kerb and drive off. Get the licence number, she told herself. She screwed up her eyes and tried to read the number plate, she could just make out the last three letters... XRT. As for the car? Was it a Rover or a Humber Hawk, she couldn't be sure. And the colour? Under the street lighting it had appeared to be black, but she couldn't be certain. She looked around, searching for the little girl, but she was nowhere to be seen.

With shoulders slumped and a sense of frustration, Cynthia walked slowly back down to the High Street to her car where Martha was waiting. What was she to tell her? And how would she react? As for the car registration number, even though she had a friend who worked at Wakefield police station, she doubted whether three letters would be sufficient to give her the name of the owner of the vehicle.

What about the little girl? Where had she sprung from? She had to be local. Cynthia had so many questions to ask her, but how to find her? She must live in the village, in which case someone must know her. Cynthia stopped in her tracks. There was one person. When she'd accepted this case the first thought she'd had was whether it could be Laura Windle up to her old tricks. But after her meeting with her this week she knew that she would never put a child at risk.

She felt a smile curve her lips. She remembered Miss Windle's offer of help. As soon as she got home she'd phone her.

Chapter Fourteen

Friday night.
9pm

Simon opened the back door, walked up the driveway to the pavement and glanced along the High Street. All was quiet, not even a straggler to be seen. They were probably all living it up in the George and Mary pub on Otley Road and unlikely to come back this way until well after closing time. So, if he was going to do a recce around Jimmy's old shop, he'd best get on with it.

He went back inside and eyed the tools he'd put out in readiness – torch, screwdriver, small crowbar, a sturdy piece of wire and, as an afterthought, a pair of bicycle clips. Perhaps he was being over cautious about the bicycle clips, he thought, as he packed the others tools into his pockets and put the clips around his trouser legs, but then again old Jimmy had stocked pet food and that often encouraged mice and rats. Best play it safe. If there was one thing that really gave him the willies, it was vermin.

He went into the living room in search of his final weapon against any potential rodents. He didn't need to look far. Goliath, his fat ginger tomcat, lay sprawled out close to the electric fire, relishing the heat. Simon grinned as he looked down at him. Cats were born survivors. They always knew where to find food and warmth. Simon pulled a canvas shoulder bag across his chest, then bending down, scooped up Goliath and put him in the bag. The cat meowed loudly in protest but he ignored him, 'Don't argue with me, Gol, we've got work to do.' He picked up his torch and walked across the road towards the empty shop.

It was the wire that did it. After trying out several old keys of his own, and fiddling with the screwdriver with no result, he decided to try the wire and began to jiggle it in the lock. After a few minutes he heard the tumblers move, swiftly followed by a satisfying click. Success! Holding his breath he gave the door a gentle push and it swung open. He entered, closing it silently behind him.

For a moment he stood in the hallway, allowing the light from his torch to guide him, then made his way to what he remembered used to be the stock room. He eased the door open and walked in.

Cardboard boxes were stacked high in the centre of the room, all of them were clearly labelled 'Fragile handle with care.' Simon grinned wryly as he read these optimistic instructions and carefully eased a corner of a box nearest to him open. It was full of Christmas baubles, so no surprises there. He was just about to peek inside another box when he heard it.

He stood stock still, clutching the bag with Goliath in it for reassurance. Yes, he could distinctly hear the scratching and the squeaking of… was it mice or, was it…? 'Think man, think!' he told himself. The squeaking was getting closer. Was it coming from the other side of the boxes? Panic seized him. He bolted out of the stockroom, across the hall and through the door opposite as fast as his legs would carry him. He was halfway down the steps before he realized he was heading towards the cellar and not the back door.

Goliath meowed loudly, struggled out of the bag and scrambled onto Simon's shoulder. He clutched the cat and froze as the beam of light from his torch shone down on a pair of bright eyes. One thing was certain, they sure weren't Goliath's. Horrified he realized that a large rat was glowering up at him from the bottom of the stairs. The sweat broke out on his face and his adrenalin surged. He did the only thing he could think of. Grabbing Goliath, he dropped him to the floor in front of the rodent and yelled 'Kill!' at the top of his voice.

Goliath, with ears back and fur bristling, took one look at the rat, let out a piercing 'Meow,' and turning tail, shot straight back upstairs. Simon tried to grab at him as he passed, but in so doing dropped his torch. There was only one thing to do in situations like this… Run!

Simon was gasping for breath when he reached the top of the steps and was about to race towards the back door of the shop when a ray of light appeared across the hallway floor, immediately followed by the sound of a vehicle pulling up outside. He stood rooted to the spot; to go back would be to confront the rat, to go to the door would mean to face up to whoever was about to enter the shop. He desperately looked around for somewhere to hide. There used to be a downstairs lavatory, didn't there? Think man, think. Where was it? He heard footsteps on the gravel outside and the sound of male voices... Voices? There must be two of them! Now came the grating of a key in the lock, which seemed to finally kick his brain into gear. He remembered; the lavatory was two doors down on the right. He crept swiftly towards it and pulling the door open, slid inside.

Simon closed the door softly, then pressed his ear against the wood. Male voices, getting louder, then fading and then the sound of another door closing. They've gone into the stockroom, he thought, now might be the time to make a break for it. Suddenly, he heard the plaintive 'meow' of Goliath – he must be close by. Simon was about to ease the door open and grab the cat when a loud voice said, 'Bloody hell, what's a flaming moggy doing in here?'

'Thought it was yours,' said the other man, 'thought you'd gone and got him to get rid of the rats.'

'Nah!' said the first voice, 'I've put poison down for that,' he gave a grim laugh, 'and if that cat's been nibbling at it, he ain't half going to get a belly ache tomorrow.' Abruptly, there came a protesting wail from Goliath and the man said, 'Out you go cat, go on gerrof home.' And the back door slammed loudly.

Simon breathed a sigh of relief; at least Goliath was out of danger. What he'd overheard about the poison was worrying though, he'd need to keep a close eye on the cat tomorrow. He turned and looked up at the small square of light that came from the window above the toilet and sighed. Even if he could get that window open he had his doubts as to whether he could squeeze through it. With his stocky build he could easily get stuck halfway. He thought about how embarrassing it would be to be found by his neighbours hanging out of the window. Or even worse, his heart thudded at the thought, if he was discovered by those two blokes.

There was nothing else for it, Simon sat down on the toilet and waited, hoping that neither of the men in the shop should feel the need to relieve themselves. Minutes felt like hours as Simon listened to footsteps going up the stairs to the flat and quickly returning. Now both voices became louder and it was clear to him that the men were in the hall near to his door.

'That's all of the stock then?' One man asked.

'More or less, I've got another delivery of fancy Christmas goods due next week and that's about it, then I'll be able to open.'

'What about the perishables?' the other man said.

Perishables? Thought Simon in horror.

'Nah! They're not due 'til two weeks before Christmas,' he laughed, 'then I'll pile 'em high and sell 'em cheap!'

Simon clapped his hand over his mouth to stop crying out in protest.

The man's companion laughed in agreement, then asked, 'how's your other little side-line getting on?'

'Oh that. That's doing nicely. It's amazing the things that these village businesses want to sweep under the carpet, but then I've always said, 'it's not who you know, it's what you know about them,' that's proving very profitable. Look, it's nearly ten o'clock already, let's not lose good drinking time. The George and Mary will be closed soon. We'd better get a move on if we want a pint or two.'

Simon listened to the back door being relocked and the vehicle driving away. He waited a few minutes longer before he made his escape, just to be sure. He went out of the door, relocked it and hurried across the street to his shop. Rushing into the living room he made a beeline for the drinks cabinet, poured himself a large whisky and gulped it down in one. Having steadied his nerves he sat down and thought about what he'd overheard.

So, the unknown trader was going to sell Christmas trees was he? Simon felt sure that's what the man had meant by 'perishables,' he'd hardly be meaning mince pies, would he now? Well, not with rats on the premises. But if the man really was going to sell Christmas trees and wreaths, Simon's jaw tightened and he sat upright, he for one was ready to meet the challenge.

He got out of his chair, refilled his glass, and went through to the kitchen to search for Goliath.

No trace of paw marks near the cat flap. He looked around in vain; he must still be outside, he thought. Walking to the door he opened it and looked out into the night.

'Go!' he called and felt a huge sense of relief as his ginger cat raced past him and into the warmth of the kitchen. Smiling, he closed the door.

As he went back into the living room the other remarks he'd overheard came into his mind. What had that bloke meant about 'other side-lines' and 'village businesses,' and having stuff 'swept under the carpet'? What else was it he'd said? Ah yes, "It's not who you know, it's what you know about them…"

Simon scowled as he thought this through. The question was, what did this bloke know about business people here in Fawdon? Whatever it was, it sounded threatening. In fact, it sounded very much like blackmail. He started as another unwelcome thought shot into his mind. Nervously he took another large gulp from his whisky – surely Miss Windle was not up to her old tricks again?

Chapter Fifteen

Saturday morning
6.45am

Alfredo eased the back door of his restaurant open with his foot as he struggled through with a stack of boxes. Crossing the kitchen, he placed the boxes of vegetables on the table then went back, closed the door and switched on the light. Returning to the table he began to unpack them.

He placed the celery and celeriac in the sink ready for preparation, then he examined the remaining vegetables with approval. Well-satisfied with his purchases from the market, he stowed them away in the larder.

It was when he was on his way back from the larder that he glanced towards the restaurant glass door and saw a figure press what looked like a paper notice on it. The figure looked up and upon seeing him, scurried away.

'What is this?' Alfredo shouted as he ran through the restaurant, brought out his keys and unlocked the door. He read the notice out loud.

'Apologies to our customers, but due to unforeseen circumstances this restaurant will be closed today.'

Alfredo read the notice again; he looked closely at the bottom of the paper but couldn't see an identification of any authority.

'Why doesn't it have any name on it?' he muttered. 'Surely if it was the Gas board or the Water board they would have informed me.' He looked around. 'So who has done this?' Angrily he tore the paper from the door. 'What unforeseen circumstances?' he said as he looked along the High Street. 'Who has the right to stick such a notice on my premises without contacting me first?'

Puzzled, Alfredo locked the restaurant door and walked slowly down the street. If it was the Gas Board or such he felt sure he would not be the only one who would be inconvenienced; perhaps he should ask at the corner newsagents, he knew that they'd be open. He was about to pass the Golden Rose Tea Shoppe when he saw a glimmer of light coming from within. He touched the glass door of the shop in the hope of seeing another notice but as he did so the door swung open. Surprised, he peered into the entrance; surely a tea shop wouldn't be open at this hour?

Taking a few cautious steps inside he called out 'Hello?' but there was no answer. Maybe something was wrong? He made his way towards the light at the rear of the café. Reaching a half closed door, he rapped politely on it then pushed it open.

The woman working in the kitchen gaped in surprise at him and almost dropped the tray of buns she was holding. 'Where on earth did you spring from?' she gasped, 'we're not open, you know.'

'I'm sorry but your shop door was open.' Alfredo said. 'I did call out.' He saw that the woman's pretty face had turned bright red and that her hands were shaking.

'Still no reason for you to come barging in here,' she said breathlessly.

Why is she so breathless? Maybe it's the heat in this kitchen.

'I'm so sorry,' he said again, 'I didn't mean to scare you. Allow me to introduce myself, I'm Alfredo and I own the restaur…'

'I know very well who *you* are,' the woman snapped, 'and I'm Martha McPherson and *I* own these premises.'

'Oh, I see!' He went towards her but she shrank back. 'It's so nice to meet you after all this time. I never have the time to take afternoon tea.' He smiled down at her. 'Perhaps you don't have the time to have Italian meals either? So at last our paths have crossed.' He reached out to shake her hand but Martha gripped the bun tray even tighter.

Alfredo felt confused, he took a step back. I've frightened her, how can I put her at her ease? Looking around the kitchen he inhaled deeply, 'Those cakes smell wonderful.' He said. But Martha did not deign to reply. He watched as she put down the tray, put butter and sugar into a mixing bowl and began to blend them together. He tried again, 'The reason that I came in here…' his voice trailed off and he licked his lips as he saw the mixture in the bowl become creamier. It reminded him of the times when, as a boy, he had watched his stepmother bake cakes, and how she'd allowed him to lick the bowl when she'd finished.

'You were saying?' Martha said sharply.

'Ah yes,' he cleared his throat. 'I found a notice stuck on my door just now and it said that I'd be closed for today due to unforeseen circumstances. I did wonder if you had received a similar notification.'

Martha shook her head, picked up another tray of buns and stared down at the kitchen table. Then, she neatly sliced the tops off the cakes in the tray and cut them in half. 'Can't say that I have,' she said as she topped the buns with butter cream. 'I only went out to see if the milk man had been.' She shot a swift glance at Alfredo, then quickly looked down at her work. 'Must have forgotten to lock the door again,' she added, almost as an afterthought.

'Easily done,' Alfredo said quietly. He felt his mouth water as he saw Martha replace the bun lids at an angle, then sprinkle them with icing sugar. His stomach rumbled loudly. 'Sorry,' he mumbled in embarrassment, 'I've not yet had breakfast.'

Martha looked up at him and for the first time Alfredo saw a twinkle in her round blue eyes. She smothered a laugh, 'You're hungry?'

'It's okay. I'll eat as soon as I get back.' His glance drifted longingly towards the tray of buns. 'What are they called?'

Martha grinned. 'Butterfly buns. I usually make them as a Saturday special.'

'You do all of the baking as well running the business?'

'No, just the odd batch or two, or the occasional special order of Bilberry pies and such. The rest of the goods I buy wholesale.'

'Such a versatile lady,' he smiled, then added quickly, 'well, I must be going. I will see whether the newsagent has received any such notice.' He gave a shrug. 'Maybe it is only for me and if it is I will phone them later and find out the meaning behind it.' He turned towards the door, 'So sorry to have troubled you.' His gaze drifted once more towards the buns.

Laughingly Martha popped three of the cakes into a bag and thrust it at him. 'Here,' she said, 'I can't bear to see a man go hungry. Have these with your breakfast and let me know what you think of them… as one professional to another.'

'So kind of you! Thank you and I will,' he broke off. 'But we will speak again.' He smiled tentatively then turned and walked out of the kitchen.

Martha watched the door close behind him. She stood motionless for a minute and listened carefully for the sound of the café door closing. Just to be sure, she hurried through the café and checked that the door really was shut before locking it and letting out a deep sigh of relief. That had been close, he'd almost caught her. Slowly she walked back towards the kitchen. Did he suspect? What would she have done if he'd accused her? Without warning she felt regret the heavy weight of regret begin to grow in the pit of her stomach.

She shouldn't have done it, he seemed such a pleasant man.

Chapter Sixteen

*Saturday morning
10.30am*

Laura Windle had just put on her coat and was about to reach for her shopping basket when the phone rang. Drat! She thought as she hurried to answer it, if that was the Vicar phoning yet again with some silly query, she would have to be firm with him. She picked up the receiver; 'Fawden 6578,' she said sharply.

'Miss Windle?' a female voice enquired.

'Yes.' Laura relaxed; this was certainly not the Vicar. 'Speaking,' she added, by way of encouragement.

'It's Cynthia Roberts here. You remember me? I came to see you earlier this week.'

'Oh, of course I do my dear, and how are things... progressing?'

'That's the reason I phoned. I'm afraid I have some more questions and I feel sure you'll be able to help.'

On hearing this Laura's interest deepened. 'Yes, of course my dear,' she said, 'how can I help you?'

'Would you mind very much if I came over to your house?' Cynthia said. 'It's not something I can discuss over the phone.'

'Please do, you would be most welcome. Shall we say 2pm this afternoon? I had intended to prune the rose bushes, but I'm sure they won't mind waiting.'

'That would be great,' Cynthia said. Then she asked. 'Would you mind very much if I brought Martha McPherson with me?'

For a second Laura hesitated, then she said, 'if you think it's necessary, my dear.'

'You sound rather puzzled at my request, but believe me, Miss Windle I have a good reason for bringing her. I'll see you this afternoon then.' There came a click and the sound of an empty line.

Laura stared down at the receiver for a moment, before slowly putting it back on its rest. She picked up her shopping basket as thoughts from the past came flooding back into her mind. She really did hope she could help Cynthia and Martha McPherson with this dreadful blackmailing business. Her sense of guilt returned. If only she had not started in the first place. If only she could remember if Julia had slipped that sheet of paper back into her handbag on that fateful day. Had the ambulance man picked it up and put it in his pocket? Or had it blown away unnoticed over the ice crusted cobbles when she had knelt by Julia and waited for the ambulance.

Laura let out a sigh of frustration and headed for the door. 'If' is the longest word in the English language,' she told herself sharply, 'now it's up to you to help Cynthia find this evil person and deal with them. You were the one who started this blackmail business three years ago, even though it was to save the life of a child. Because of that you must take the consequences. You must help finish it.'

Chapter Seventeen

Saturday
10am

Martha opened the till drawer and tipped the little plastic bags of coins into the correct compartments. She frowned as she reached for the bag that contained the silver coins – these new-fangled five penny pieces were so tiny and confusing, her customers were always mistaking them for the old sixpences which didn't exist anymore. She sighed, they'd have to get used to them, she supposed, there'd be no going back now. Decimal currency was here to stay now that they were going to join the European Union next year.

She placed the notes in the till then closed the drawer and put the plastic bags away. Of course what she missed most of all were the small octagonal three penny bit coins, there was no mistaking them, but they were gone forever, like so much else in this world.

The phone rang, disturbing her train of thought. She walked into her office and picked up the receiver. 'Golden Rose Tea Shoppe,' she announced.

'Mrs McPherson, is that you?'

'Speaking,' said Martha who was already wondering if it was one of her part-time waitresses about to call in sick.

'It's Cynthia Roberts here. Look I know it's short notice but can you be ready to come out with me at 1.45pm today? It really is important.'

Martha felt panicky; Saturday was the busiest day of the week. Her mind raced, this would mean having to ask an extra part-time waitress to come in and help out. She said, 'Well yes I can, but I'll need to call in more staff first.' She thought for a moment then asked. 'Where are we going?'

'I'm taking you to visit Miss Laura Windle. I'm not sure if you know her, but she is one of the few people who just may be able to help us find that little girl from last night.'

At the reminder of last night's happening's Martha's heart began to pound, she'd been so scared and then the fact that the blackmailer had actually sent a little girl to do his dirty work had somehow made it ten times worse.

'You still there?' asked Cynthia.

'Yes,' Martha said anxiously, 'but I've not heard anything from the blackmailer yet. I mean what's going to happen now that he knows the money wasn't there?'

'We'll deal with that when it happens.' Cynthia said. 'So I'll pick you up this afternoon?'

'Right,' said Martha, 'I'll see you then.' She put the phone back on its rest. She thought for a moment, then picked the receiver up again and began to dial. She'd need to call in Sally, the other part-time waitress; knowing her, she'd be glad of the extra work.

*

1.40pm.

Martha stood at the back of the café and watched the girls busily serving their customers. The café was almost full and Martha felt reluctant to leave. Her instinct was to stay and help the waitresses, rather than abandoning them at the busiest time of the day. She pulled her coat sleeve back and looked again at her watch, just another few minutes and then Cynthia would be here. Her thoughts returned to Miss Windle, she knew that one or two people in the village actually called Miss Windle by her first name, Laura, but they were few and far between. In fact she was well known as being Fawdon's righteous do-gooder. Indeed, some villagers had been known to cross the street just to avoid her.

With a sigh, Martha strolled towards the café door and peered out. She liked Laura Windle. Indeed, thinking back to this summer, she felt indebted to her. It had been on a day as busy as this when one of her waitresses had slipped and cut her arm badly. There's been spilt tea and blood all over the floor and had it not been for Miss Windle quietly standing up and giving the girl first aid, whilst she was desperately phoning the ambulance, heaven only knows what would have happened.

When the ambulance men did arrive and the girl was safely on her way to the hospital, Martha had gone back into the café only to find that Miss Windle had dealt with the other customers and that everything had been cleared and tidied away. Martha smiled in reminiscence, she would always be grateful to Miss Windle for that. The short blast of a car horn outside the café brought Martha's thoughts hurtling back into the present. That must be Cynthia. She called a hasty goodbye to the staff and made her way towards the door.

Chapter Eighteen

Saturday
1.55pm

Laura Windle stood in the kitchen and started to set out the tea tray in preparation for her visitors. Carefully she selected the bone china tea set with the blue forget-me-not pattern and placed it gently on the tray, closely followed by the sugar and the milk jug. She thought for a moment, went to her larder and got out the shortbread biscuits. As Martha McPherson was Scottish she felt they would be appropriate. Once more she checked that everything was in readiness, that the room was warm enough, that the settee cushions were fluffed up and that the kettle was on the hob, then she walked over to the window to await the arrival of her guests.

As she stood there she recalled what she knew about the owner of the Golden Rose Tea Shoppe. Martha McPherson was attractive and in her mid-forties, so still quite young. She was certainly hard working, a good baker and an efficient business woman. Apart from the recent blackmail threat that Cynthia had told her about, Laura had never heard of any scandal about her. Except…

Laura frowned as a distant memory popped into her mind. One could hardly call it scandal though. There had been one rather upsetting incident which had occurred... when was it? Yes, now she remembered. She had been having tea in the café with the Fawdoners Gardening Group when the man...

Yes, well that must have been more than two years ago now. It had certainly been in the summer because she remembered thinking that it might have been better to have ordered lemonade instead of boiling hot tea, but then Julia had insisted. Laura clicked her tongue as she remembered; that was one of the most annoying things about Julia, she was bossy and she never had the least consideration for anyone else's feelings. Now, she told herself, forget about Julia. What was it about the man? He'd lurched into the café looking angry and she was almost certain that he had been inebriated. He'd shouted at the poor waitress, demanding to see his wife. A white faced Martha McPherson had appeared in the café and hastily guided him into her office. Even though Martha had closed the office door behind her, she could not help but overhear the shouts and the dreadful language that came from within. The whole incident had not lasted more than a few minutes before the husband, his face dark with fury, had staggered back thorough the café and out on to the street. Laura remembered feeling uncomfortable. She'd listened and tried in vain to hear what was being said in the office, but it was unclear, so she'd sipped her tea politely and wondered.

There came the sound of a car pulling up outside. Laura recognised the grey Ford Escort and saw Cynthia and Martha coming down the path. Smiling, she went into the hall and opened the door to greet them.

*

A few minutes later Laura sat and watched the two ladies sipping their tea. She noticed that Martha, who had seemed wary at first, had begun to relax as she leaned back against the settee cushions. Laura's gaze drifted on to Cynthia who was leaning forward and trying hard not to look at the shortbread biscuits on the tray. She had refused them firmly when Laura had first offered them to her, but now? Laura smiled; she could see that Cynthia was having difficulty resisting temptation.

She cleared her throat and said tactfully. 'This is so pleasant to see you both here. I don't often get visitors on a Saturday afternoon.'

Cynthia placed her cup and saucer on the coffee table and said, 'It's good to be here.' She looked at Martha. 'Have I your permission to tell Miss Windle what happened last night? Why we're here and how it all came about?'

Martha said nervously, 'Well yes, if you think it will help.' She leaned forward and said to Laura, 'I'm being blackmailed y'see and whichever awful person is responsible must have made a little girl collect the bag I left.'

Laura Windle said firmly, 'Could you, perhaps, describe the little girl to me?'

'Martha only glimpsed her briefly,' Cynthia said, 'but I caught her and I know what she looked like. She was about nine or ten years of age, very thin, height about 4 foot 9 inches. She had big eyes, an elfin face and darkish curly hair.' Cynthia thought for a second then added, 'course the kid's hair might have been dirty, a good shampoo might make her hair blonde.'

'Nine to ten years old,' Laura pondered, 'she'd still be at the village school then.' She got up, went to fetch a notebook and pen, then sat down and entered the child's details carefully.

'Clearly the blackmailer had bribed her into collecting the money from the bowling green,' Cynthia said, 'and he'd chosen well, that kid could run like a hare.'

'So the blackmailer got the money?' Laura asked sharply.

'No, not a chance! What he got was a bag full of paper.'

'I'll bet he's going to get me for that,' Martha muttered uneasily, 'any time now I'm sure he's going to have another shot at me.'

'Might I ask,' Laura interrupted cautiously, 'why someone is blackmailing you.'

Martha chewed on her lip and shot a glance at Cynthia.

'I can assure you that anything you tell me about this matter will always be treated in the strictest confidence,' Laura said.

Cynthia nodded her encouragement. 'Tell her Martha, your secret's safe with Miss Windle.'

Laura leaned back in her chair and listened to Martha's tale. From time to time she made notes but continued to let her talk without interruption. When she had finished Laura looked at Cynthia for confirmation, but saw that she was staring at the carpet, frowning. 'Is there perhaps something that Martha may have missed out?' she asked.

'That's just what I've been thinking,' Cynthia replied. She turned to Martha and said, 'I can't get away from the feeling that you're not telling me everything. You are a strong competent woman and at the time you probably loved your husband.'

Martha shook her head vigorously, 'No, not on your life, the romance in our relationship had disappeared a long time before.'

'Then why did you commit perjury for him?' Cynthia interrupted.

'I told you. He was a drinker. He worked as a driver in long distance haulage. If he'd been convicted he'd have lost his job.'

'It might have been a good thing if he had been convicted,' Cynthia said. 'No one wants a drunken truck driver on the road and besides, there are other jobs.'

'You just don't understand, there were other reasons.'

'What other reasons?' Cynthia insisted. 'Tell us.' She saw that Martha was close to tears.

'All right then,' Martha sniffed, 'Bert was a bully, he'd been a lovely man when I first married him but then the drink got to him and with it came the...' She stopped, choked back a sob, fished a hanky from her pocket and blew her nose loudly.

'Came what?' prompted Cynthia.

'The beatings! He knocked me around when he was drunk. I couldn't tell anyone 'cause when he was sober he was such a charmer. But then when he thought he could be sent down he...' She hesitated and dabbed at her nose worriedly.

'Go on,' urged Cynthia.

'Held a razor to my throat,' Martha blurted, 'said if I didn't lie for him he'd finish me when he came out.' She fingered the side of her neck. 'If you look you can see a faint scar... I was terrified, I daren't tell anyone.'

There was a long silence before Cynthia said, 'For heaven's sake! I just knew there was something you weren't telling me. Why on earth didn't you call the police?'

'And have to tell them why he was threatening me? If that all becomes public now and the press gets hold of it, not only will I be charged with perjury and the case reopened, but if he gets wind of it, my life won't be worth living.'

Cynthia said quietly, 'I see. Then we must make sure that doesn't happen.'

Laura leaned forward and touched Martha's hand reassuringly. 'We will do our utmost to help you, my dear.' She turned to Cynthia. 'I will try and find out just who that little girl was. It might well mean looking for a needle in a proverbial haystack, but I will persevere and I will be in touch with you as soon as I have any news.' She put the empty cups and saucers neatly back on the tray, then hesitated and enquired politely. 'More tea anyone, or perhaps a biscuit?

Cynthia smiled and got to her feet. 'No thank you, we've taken up enough of your time already, Miss Windle.' She looked at her watch, 'thank you so much for listening to us.' She turned towards the door.

Martha stood up and clasped Miss Windle's hands. 'Thank you so much, I needed to tell someone the real truth.'

'I hope I can do more than just listen,' Laura said as she went out with them to the car, 'and I think you made the right decision when you asked Cynthia to help you.'

Laura stood on the path and gave a gentle wave as the two women drove off, then she hurried back into the warmth of the house. As she did so a thought occurred to her and she clicked her tongue in annoyance – she had forgotten to ask Cynthia about Peter Greystone. Surely he could not be yet another victim?

'Everything comes in threes,' she whispered to herself, 'even bad news.' She tried to dismiss her own words, but they lingered. Just to reassure herself, she made a mental note to phone Cynthia this evening and ask about him.

But first things first; as she crossed the living room she picked up her notebook and re-read the notes she had made about the little girl. 'Yes,' she said, 'on Monday I'll have a discreet word with the Headmistress at the village school.' She frowned as her thoughts moved on to Martha McPherson and the difficult situation she was in.

She knew that Cynthia would do all that she could to catch this wicked blackmailer, and she was determined to help them.

*

Cynthia watched as Martha got out of the car, gave a quick wave, and hurried into the Golden Rose Tea Shoppe; then, deep in thought, she drove off towards her own house. Martha's problem was really a lot worse than she'd expected. She'd known that Martha was not telling her everything, but to at last discover that Martha's husband was violent and a potential murderer, really was worrying. She wasn't sure how she would deal with it. Perhaps, she thought, as she drove the car into the garage, it might be a good idea to phone her old bosses and ask for their advice.

She went into in to the kitchen, took off her jacket and looked at the clock – 3.45pm. That left her plenty of time to have a shower and a sandwich before joining Peter at the old Mallins mill at 7.30pm.

She crossed over to the window, saw that it was starting to drizzle and wished she could take the car in this weather, but she'd realized from last night's experience that her motor bike would be more efficient. Also should the little girl reappear again, she was sure that she wouldn't recognise her in her biker's gear.

Chapter Nineteen

Saturday
7pm

Peter looked up at the grandfather clock in his shop and checked that it synchronized with his wrist watch. 'Yes, spot on,' he muttered, 'soon be time to go.' He stood for a moment listening to the ticking of the clock; it seemed to be in rhythm with his thumping heart. He thought about his forthcoming rendezvous with the blackmailer and his mouth tightened into an angry line. No way was he going to let that bastard get away with taking his money, he'd paid the price for his wrong-doing, he'd done his time.

His mind went back to those dreadful days behind bars. He'd taken many a beating inside, but as with all experiences, he'd learned from them. True he'd learned the hard way, but in order to survive he'd also picked up one or two tricks. He gave a grim smile as he looked down at his recent handiwork and stroked his homemade knuckle duster lightly. They say that necessity is the mother of invention; whoever would have thought that such a weapon would prove so useful to him one day. He picked it up and flexed his fingers around it. It felt comfortable in his grip and if push came to shove... Would he really be able to use it? He sighed and looked once more at the grandfather clock, watching as minute by minute, time ticked by.

*

7.15pm

He'd better phone his wife. He dialled the number and stood for a while listening to the ring tone. Should he tell Helen? How would she and the girls react if he did? Surely it was better to first catch the blackmailer tonight and tell them when it was over and done with. On hearing his wife's voice, he reached a decision.

'It's me, love. Sorry, I'm going to be late tonight... yes I know I'm late already, but I've got a customer who can't pick up his repair until about 8 o'clock.' He listened patiently to the outburst of complaints. When she'd finished he said calmly. 'Yes, I know dear, but business is business. This was an expensive repair and he is a good customer, I'll get home as soon as I can.' He replaced the receiver firmly. He had done the right thing, there was no point in telling Helen he was being blackmailed, she and the girls would only worry themselves sick.

He pulled on his coat, picked up the bulky brown envelope and eased it carefully into his pocket, then he looked at the knuckle duster again and decided to take that as well. He knew that he wasn't Muhammad Ali, but at least this way he'd be prepared. Tight lipped he strode towards the shop door and turned the sign to closed, before pulling down the blinds. Then, with an odd sense of finality, he locked it behind him.

Chapter Twenty

Saturday
Time 7.22pm

Cynthia rode through the drizzling rain until she reached the burned out ruins of Mallins Mill. 'What a lousy night to arrange a meeting,' she grumbled. Cautiously she looked about her, she needed to find somewhere to hide the bike, get some shelter from the rain and, more importantly, go unnoticed. Across the cobbled street she saw an old warehouse, it looked like it was derelict as well, but it stood slightly back from the street and it was deep in shadow. 'Good,' she said, 'that'll do.' She rode the bike over and parked it close up against the warehouse wall so that the eaves from the roof gave her shelter from the rain. With relief she removed her goggles and helmet and put them in the saddle bag, then she wiped her face and pushed back some wet strands of hair.

She could see the ruins better now and she peered in the darkness at the luminous numbers on her watch – 7.27pm. Just a few more minutes to wait.

The rain increased and with it came the wind, gusting and blowing across the deserted road in waves. Cynthia leaned close against the wall and stared across the street at the old burnt out ruins. She began to feel uneasy. It was not that she believed in ghosts or silly village gossip, but now the tales about Mallins Mill came unbidden into her mind. Many of the villagers swore it was haunted by the man who set fire to it all those years ago. Some said he'd done it because he'd lost his job there and couldn't find work, so he'd torched the mill before hanging himself on the remaining beams a few days later. Cynthia shivered, she remembered that folk said on a winter's night you could hear the creaking of the old timbers as if they were groaning from some unexpected weight.' She started; was that a shadow moving through the ruins across the street? What was it? Was it a cat… or a fox? Maybe it was the wind gusting in the rain? Surely it wasn't a human? Her heart pounded. She should investigate, shouldn't she? She hesitated. She'd have to pick her way over the cobbled road and through the wet grass to the old stone slabs that were in front of the burned out old mill. It would be so easy to stumble and as for her boots…

Taking a deep breath she was about to cross the street when she saw the slight figure of Peter striding towards the ruins. He walked briskly, even jauntily towards the arranged place and Cynthia felt surprised. She'd half expected him to be timid in his approach. Perhaps he felt confident because she'd phoned him this afternoon and he knew she would be here. She watched as Peter approached the entrance to the Mill and gently placed a bulky envelope where the blackmailer had stated. Then he turned and began to walk away.

Cynthia frowned, she stared hard at the envelope, it seemed much bulkier that it should be, even if it really did contain the correct amount of money. Her thoughts were interrupted by the sound of someone singing. This was accompanied by shrill female laughter as a couple – the woman wearing a hooded plastic raincoat and the man similarly dressed in a plastic mackintosh and flat cap – came towards her. They staggered past her hiding place with their arms entwined about each other and on towards the entrance of the mill.

"I was born under a rambling star," the man bawled out tunelessly.

'Yes, you is a star, my lovely boy,' the woman screeched loudly. 'My star, my moon and my sun...'ere, don't shove like that, I nearly fell over... I reckon I'm gonna to be sick."

"I was born, and I love my Ma." the man sang on regardless, "and I've wandered far... Oy! Don't you dare spew up on me, you daft mare! Get over there by the grass.' The couple lurched ever nearer to where the envelope lay.

Drunk at this hour? They must have been to some early Christmas party. Cynthia glared at them. 'Ramble on, for heaven's sake,' she muttered through gritted teeth. 'Just get the hell out of the way.'

'But you *is* my lovely lad, aren't you,' the woman insisted, ''cause I do love you, you know.'

Without warning the man stumbled close to the envelope and, quick as a snake, snatched it up.

But, as he grabbed it a piercing alarm rang out and he spun round and dropped it.

Cynthia darted forward but the woman turned and bolted straight at her, knocking her aside. Cynthia staggered, then turned to watch the woman race off into the night, her high heels click clacking as she ran. For one split second Cynthia stood undecided, she wanted to run after the woman but she remembered the envelope and the blackmailer. She was about to retrieve it when she saw Peter running towards them. He charged straight at the man and floored him in a rugby tackle.

Gaping in amazement Cynthia watched as Peter pinned the man to the ground. Who would have thought? Peter was clearly capable of dealing with him, but what about the woman? She'd run off in the direction of the village. Racing across the road for her bike Cynthia leapt on it and set off after her. 'She can't have gone far,' she muttered. She listened to the distant echo of the woman's high heels then revved the bike into action.

As she rode through the village, Cynthia's mind returned to Peter and she wondered if she should have stayed to help him. But she reassured herself with the fact that Peter looked as if he could handle it and if they could catch both the man and the woman? That would solve everything.

*

Peter felt triumphant – he'd won! He looked down at his opponent lying helpless on the cobbled street and felt for the knuckle duster in his pocket. He tried to grab at it but his fingers slipped and in the same instant, the man started to move. Peter reached down, dragged the man to his feet and swiftly tried to force the his arm behind his back.

'I've got you now you thieving bastard,' he snarled, 'I'm going to show you what I do with rats like you.' But something struck him with terrific force on his temple and as the blackness came, his last thought was, 'wrist watch on his right hand must mean...'

*

The man staggered to his feet and looked down at his unconscious opponent. 'That'll sort him for a while,' he growled. On hearing the revving of a motor bike he looked along the street and saw it setting off in the same direction as Claire. He peered again through the rain. Under the distant street lights all he could make out was the rider's mass of curly hair; it looked to be a sort of brown gingery colour, but it was hard to tell. One thing was certain though; the rider was hot on the trail of Claire. There was no time to lose. The man raced down the road, into a side street and got into the car he'd parked there earlier, speeding off towards Claire's house. As he reached Westdown Road he switched off the lights, parked a few yards along from the house and waited. He did not have to wait long. Within minutes the running figure of Claire came into view and she darted straight into her house. The motor cyclist, riding without lights, followed a few seconds behind her. As the biker came closer and near to the street lights he could see that the rider was a woman.

*

Cynthia switched off the engine and waited. Had the woman realized that she was being followed and used the garden as a place to hide? She sat silently astride her bike, she would soon find out. After a few minutes a light came on in one of the downstairs rooms of the house and she smiled in relief. Now she knew where the woman's bolt hole was, or even more than likely this was where she lived. Her thoughts returned to Peter. She really shouldn't have left him to deal with the man on his own, even though he seemed to be more than a match for the blackmailer. But Peter was her client and it was her job to protect him. She switched on the engine and tried to control her anxiety; best get back to him as quickly as she could.

*

As the man stared at the motor cyclist a distant memory stirred in the foggy periphery of his mind. He'd seen this woman somewhere before, he was certain of it. Then it finally clicked – she'd been running after that kid who'd picked up the envelope for him the other night and he'd had to make a hasty getaway. So who the hell was she? And why was she interfering in his business?

He needed to know more. He watched her ride off again a few minutes later. Then he followed.

*

As Cynthia returned to the old mill ruins there didn't seem to be anyone in sight. Had Peter dragged the man off somewhere? She peered through the rain and the mist, calling out loudly.

'Peter?' She heard a faint groan in response and immediately swung the bike's headlight in that direction. It picked out a dark shape in the grass, just by the entrance of the mill. Cynthia jumped off the bike and ran towards the crumpled figure.

'Peter? What the hell happened?'

Grasping at her for support, Peter struggled slowly to his feet. 'Got over-confident, didn't I,' he groaned. 'Nearly had him in an arm lock and never realized he was a south paw. The rotten sod whacked me with a cobble stone.'

Cynthia peered closely at him. She could see the blood trickling down the side of his face. 'Oh my Lord, let's get you home.'

'No!' Peter protested. 'I don't want my Helen to see me like this.'

She stared at him. 'You mean she doesn't know about you being blackmailed?'

'Course not,' Peter said, 'she'd only worry.' He swayed unsteadily and clutched at Cynthia for support.

'You could come to my house and I could clean you up a bit, but...' she peered again at the wound on his temple. 'Peter, my worry is that you may have concussion.' She hesitated, 'Do you feel well enough to ride pillion? Because I think we'd best get to the Emergency Unit over at the Leeds Infirmary. Or I could go home and bring the car if you don't feel up to the bike?'

'I'm going to be fine,' Peter said irritably. 'I'll just go back to my shop.'

'Peter, you need an x-ray,' Cynthia insisted.

'Alright then, I'll get on the back. I'm just wondering what I can tell Helen.'

'You'll think of something,' Cynthia said, 'now hold tight.'

*

11.30pm

The man sat huddled up in his car on Frith Street and watched as a few yards away, the motor cyclist rode the bike into a garage. He peered bleary eyed as she then went into the house and switched on the lights.

Was she home at long last, he wondered, or was she about to go out again. She'd nearly fooled him earlier when she visited the Emergency room at Leeds Infirmary for over an hour, then out she'd come with the bloke who now had his head all bandaged. She'd then dropped the watchmaker bloke off at his shop. He'd thought then that she lived there with him and he'd been just about to drive off when out she'd come again and now here she was outside a house on Frith Road. Was this her final destination? He bloody well hoped so.

He sank back in the driving seat and felt the pain and the cold seep through him. He was almost certain he'd cracked a rib and his knuckles were in a right state. But he'd not dared going into the Emergency Unit in case the bloke recognised him. He lit up another cigarette and waited a few minutes more, just in case. Then taking a pencil from his pocket he wrote the number and address of the house on the back of the cigarette pack. He thought about Claire and grimaced. No doubt the silly bitch would be borderline hysterical by now, he just hoped she'd not been daft enough to phone the police.

With a sigh he started up the engine, best get back and reassure her before she did something stupid. He glared again at the house in Frith Street. That was the last time that interfering biker would get in his way.

Chapter Twenty One

Sunday Morning
Cynthia's office

Cynthia sat at her desk and sighed, dozens of queries and so many bills. She checked the mail again and tossed the advertising flyers in the wastepaper basket. That was the problem when she had to do extra surveillance work at night. She'd been arriving late for work in the mornings and so she'd only dealt with the really urgent problems. She stretched, raising her arms towards the ceiling and massaging the back of her neck. How she wished that Harry was still with her to give her some advice, although she already knew what he'd say;

'This'll never do, Cynth, love. You've got to be more disciplined, you'll lose clients if you're not more efficient.' He was right and she knew it, but what she really needed was a bit more support.

Wearily, she signed the cheques for the outstanding bills, put them in envelopes and placed them in her out tray ready for posting. Then with reluctance she got out the file on Martha McPherson and stared down at the printed sheet in front of her. As she did so, Martha's words from Saturday echoed round inside her head. 'He threatened to kill me if he got sent down.'

Cynthia remembered looking closely at the faint scar on the left side of Martha's neck and she'd known that the woman was not lying. Martha's husband could be a killer. If only Martha had reported him to the police for attempted murder, but she hadn't and now someone had found out about her perjury.

Cynthia stared at the phone, she needed some advice but she was reluctant to call her former bosses and all her contacts in the police force would be honour bound to report anything untoward. The phone rang, suddenly making her jump. Who would be ringing her here on a Sunday? She picked up the receiver and gave her usual greeting.

'Cynthia Roberts, private investigator.'

'Ha! At last I've found you,' said a male voice in her ear.

'Who is this?'

'"They seek her here, they seek her there. They seek this woman everywhere." Just where have you been Cynthia Roberts? Don't you recognise my voice? Should do if you're as good a P.I as people say you are.'

'Neill!' Cynthia laughed, 'Neill Collinson. Of course! How are you?'

'All the better now that I've found you,' he replied.

'Cut the flattery, Neill,' Cynthia laughed. 'Just what have you been up to? It must be over a year since...'

'Oh what with one thing and another I've been up to my eyes in work. You know how it is with insurance claims, you have to be so thorough when you're investigating them. In many ways it's a lot more difficult than your job.'

'Come off it Neill, I earn my daily crust. Butv how on earth did you find me?'

'Don't ask such silly questions Cynth. I am an insurance investigator. I checked with your former bosses and they gave me your Fawdon address and phone number. I've been calling that number dozens of times and you're never there. So, I had another think and checked with yellow pages and voila!'

Cynthia felt a sense of pleasure on hearing Neill's voice. In her early days of training she'd met him through her bosses, as they often had to coordinate with the insurance companies. Neill had been kind to her and had often quietly taught her a few tricks in the art of self-defence. He'd had dinner with her and Harry a few times in the past and Harry had liked him. 'That man's got lots of common sense,' he'd remarked.

'Cynth? You still there?'

'I was just trying to remember when it was I last saw you.'

'Far too long as far as I'm concerned. Now listen Cynth, I know you'll be very busy what with a new business and all, but have you got time for a drink and a bite to eat? What about your local in Fawdon? It's the George and Mary on Otley Road, isn't it?'

'How did you know that?'

'Another silly question, it's my job. How about Wednesday night around seven?'

'You're up to something, I know it. But yes, I'd love to meet up with you, just give me your number.' She quickly glanced at her desk diary. 'Yes, I'm clear for here, but just to be sure when I get home I'll check my calendar for Wednesday evening and get back to you.'

'Right then,' he gave her his number then said, 'looking forward to catching up with you, Cynth. I'll see you Wednesday.' And he was gone.

*

Cynthia replaced the receiver slowly. It had been great to hear from Neill, he was such a nice man, but, the thought lingered, he was also an insurance investigator who specialised in investigating fire damage claims. So while it would be wonderful to meet up with an old friend again, she was sure there was more to the invitation then just catching up and reminiscing about old times.

The phone rang again sharply.

Cynthia snatched up the receiver, 'Now what, Neill?'

'I do beg your pardon,' said a polite female voice in her ear, 'I am trying to contact a Mrs Cynthia Roberts.'

'Miss Windle,' Cynthia said, on recognising the voice, 'I'm so sorry, it's me.'

'Cynthia? Then I did dial the correct number after all, I am relieved.'

Cynthia felt puzzled. 'Is there a problem Miss Windle?'

'Of course you must be wondering why I am calling you, especially on a Sunday. I hope you will forgive me for intruding and calling you at your office on your rest day. I could not get an answer from your home phone, so I assumed that you would be at work.'

'You were right, Miss Windle. I'm here trying to catch up on some paper work. Now how can I help you?'

'I do apologise, but I forgot to ask you about Peter Greystone, I remembered that you mentioned you were going to visit him last week.' There came a pause and then Miss Windle continued. 'You see I have been thinking a lot about him. Such a nice quiet little man and so hard working. Please put my mind at rest and tell me that my suspicions are wrong and he has not become victim number three?'

Cynthia sighed deeply. 'I'm afraid he has, in fact I can tell you that he met up with the blackmailer last night...'

There came a gasp from the other end of the phone.

Cynthia continued. 'The good news is the blackmailer did not get the money. The bad news, however, is that Peter ended up in the Emergency Unit at Leeds Infirmary but he's alright now,' she added hastily. 'To cut a long story short, there was a fight and the blackmailer escaped.'

She was about to ask Miss Windle what made her think of Peter and to ask her thoughts on the woman in the plastic raincoat who had accompanied the blackmailer, but before she could speak Miss Windle interrupted her.

'Cynthia, there is something I simply must tell you. I do not know if you remember a Mrs Julia Barnes, a friend of mine... she was killed accidentally two years ago?'

Cynthia thought back. She had never been really interested in Miss Windle's friends and at that time, for reasons of her own, she had regarded Miss Windle with anger and resentment. But she could recall a tall, gangly figure with a cut glass accent, who frequently accompanied Miss Windle and was often to be seen teetering around the village on outrageously high heels. 'I think I know the person you mean,' she said, 'I didn't know that she'd died though.'

'Yes,' said Miss Windle, rather gloomily. 'She is gone... but she is not forgotten,' she said, her voice becoming slightly more cheerful. She gave a deep sigh, 'I have to tell you that Julia Barnes found out about my little 'business' and I can only say that for reasons of greed she tried to force me into a partnership along similar lines with her.'

'You mean another type of blackmailing business?'

'Yes, but this time based on profit and not charity. On the day of the charity walk we argued about it and I, of course, refused to join her in her most dishonest venture.'

'Well jolly good for you,' Cynthia interrupted.

'I have not quite finished, my dear,' Miss Windle reproved her gently. 'You see, on the day in question, Julia had prepared a list.' She hesitated then said quickly, 'a list upon which were many of the villager's names and, as I recall, the names of two of them were Mr Lawrence, of 'Lorenzo's Restaurant,' and Mrs McPherson, of The Golden Rose Tea Shoppe. My fear is that there may have also been the name of Peter Greystone, but more worrying still is that there were many more.'

Cynthia sat bolt upright in her chair on hearing this. She clutched the receiver tightly. 'Miss Windle,' she said. 'Where is the list?'

'I wish I knew. Julia was holding it on the day of the accident. I remember it was windy and snowing. It was either blown away when the truck hit her or...'

'Or what?'

'It could be somewhere in Julia's old house, or in her handbag that the ambulance man picked up and placed on the stretcher. You see my dear, all of Julia's clothes and such were returned to her sister after she had passed away. I do have the keys to her house but all of her personal things are in boxes in the attic and I am reluctant to rifle through them.'

'So in fact this list could be anywhere, if it even exists.' Cynthia interrupted.

'There is no doubt of its existence, your clients' names were on the list.'

'Then our first port of call should be to look in Julia Barnes' old house.'

'I think so, I'm sure you know the house? It's a Victorian semi-detached on the corner of Westdown Road. Julia's sister inherited it.'

A light went on in Cynthia's mind. Only last night she'd followed the rain coated woman to a house on Westdown Road. 'Does Julia Barnes's sister live in the house now?'

'Oh, yes. She moved in about three weeks ago. She's a blonde haired lady, not a bit like Julia… quite unfriendly really. One cannot help but notice the alterations she has made to the house and garden and, I have to say, not quite to my taste at all.'

'This needs looking into,' Cynthia said, ignoring Miss Windle's pointless remarks. 'What is the lady's name?'

'Claire Forbes,' Miss Windle replied. 'Yes, I have to agree, not that I would wish to point the finger of blame at anyone. There may not be any connection.'

'Of course not,' said Cynthia as she scribbled the name down. 'But I think she needs checking out.'

There came a deep sigh of relief from the other end of the line. 'You are right my dear and I hope that you will keep me informed of any developments?'

'I sure will, Miss Windle.'

'And if I can help at all?'

'I'll get back to you as soon as I have further news.'

'Then I will say goodbye and let you get on with your work.' There was a click as the line disconnected.

Cynthia sat staring at the receiver, trying to digest the information Miss Windle had given her. What had started off as three blackmail cases, which was bad enough, was now becoming more and more complicated. One thing was certain, tomorrow she would have to investigate this Claire Forbes and, if possible, somehow find that blasted list before even more blackmail cases appeared.

Chapter Twenty Two

Monday morning
6am

Martha walked through the café towards the front door and unlocked it. Looking out into the darkness of the High Street she bent down and picked up the small milk crate on the door step, then stared at it in surprise. Along with the five bottles of milk needed for the café there was another bottle, a bottle of Chianti. She brought the milk crate indoors then picked up the Chianti and examined it. Attached to it was a card. It read *'To the lady with the butterfly buns, your cakes were delicious so please accept this little offering from me with my thanks.'* It was signed *'Alfredo.'*

Martha stared at the words for a moment and as she did so, she felt her face flush. How nice of the man to think of her and all because of the few buns she'd given him. She smiled as she locked the café door again, before drifting dreamily back to her kitchen. She thought again about their meeting on Saturday – he was such a charming man and she had been so rude to him. But then, she thought defensively, many men were charmers and she was sure he had been spying.

'Because of what you had done,' a voice in her head reminded her, *'to say nothing about what you did last week.'*

'That was different,' she muttered to herself. 'Business is business and I thought he was the enemy. He still could be.'

'Only if you make it so,' the voice argued. Martha hesitated; perhaps there might be a way to be friends? Some sort of compromise. Maybe she could talk to him about the two businesses.

She smiled again as she thought about Alfredo, with his chocolate brown eyes, and he must have really liked her baking. She strolled towards the cooker and put the kettle on. She'd phone him later in the day of course, but first things first. She was just about dying for a cup of tea.

Five minutes later as she sipped her drink, her thoughts went back to Saturday's meeting with Cynthia Roberts and Miss Windle, and the doubts returned to her mind. Should she really have told them about Bert, her ex-husband? She still felt unsure, but she knew that as soon as she had told them, she'd felt a great relief. Almost as though a great weight had been lifted from her shoulders. She'd lived with the fear of this man for so long. Heaven only knew what she would do if he were to come back into her life. And what about the blackmailer – he'd not got the money this time, but she knew he'd not let her get away with it. Sooner or later, he'd be back with a vengeance.

She shivered and finished her tea, then put the cup in the sink. There was no point in worrying there was work to be done. The café would be open in a couple of hours and there were sandwiches to make up. She went to the fridge and got out the ingredients. As she began buttering the bread, she told herself to think of something nice and so she thought again about Alfredo. She smiled; it would be good to have another chat with him.

Chapter Twenty Three

Monday morning
10.30am

Laura strode briskly out of the school playground and made sure that she had closed the gates securely behind her. The time was close to morning break and it would never do to have some child escapee seize the chance to dash home.

She turned right into South View Road and made her way towards the High Street. Although she walked quickly and nodded politely to other villagers as she met them, her mind was occupied with her recent interview with the new Headmistress, a Mrs Mary Smithson.

As Laura thought about this lady, her mouth turned down. How things had changed since her days in school. It was not that this woman was unhelpful, but the very sight of her sitting on the edge of her desk and swinging her legs in an unseemly manner was really most distracting. What had happened to discipline in schools these days? Still, she had managed to get most of the information she needed. The name of the little girl who seemed to fit Cynthia's description was Penny-Ann Leeming, daughter of Marilyn Leeming. Laura smiled wryly, she remembered Marilyn well. That girl always had her head stuck in a film star magazine and was forever at the Saturday cinema matinees.

It seemed, so the Headmistress had told her, that Penny was about to follow in her mother's star-struck footsteps. She was certainly not academically endowed, although on the plus side, according to the Headmistress, she was an excellent athlete – top of her class in running and hurdles. However, it would seem that she was also an expert in playing truant.

The problem was that Penny's mother did shift work down at the Otley Bus Depot and as she was a single parent, it was hard to keep Penny under control. Of course the truant officer had been notified and hopefully, the Headmistress added, this truancy would soon be put to an end.

Laura had not commented on hearing this remark. She knew from past experience that a visit from the truant officer would usually have little effect, especially if both parents worked all day. However, one thing was in her favour, she knew Marilyn Leeming and was almost certain that she still lived at the same address. She would need to think about the right time to visit her. Perhaps when school finished for the day would be best? Meanwhile she had other business to attend to.

She hurried on past the Vicarage and made a sharp left into Green Lane where the Church Hall was situated. As she came through the doors she could already hear the buzz of female chatter emanating from the kitchen. She smiled, Advent is here now and there is much to prepare.

For a while she stood quietly watching the women putting up the garlands in the hall. She had debated with the vicar as to when they should put up the Christmas tree. She would have liked to have had it done this week, but the vicar had said it was too early. 'The playgroup might damage the baubles and that tinsel stuff gets everywhere,' he'd complained.

Laura had fought back her indignation at his remarks. She had wanted to remind him what Christmas was all about. She loved to see the faces of the little ones when they looked at the brightly coloured Christmas tree, especially the toddlers. They would sit there looking up at the tree, their tiny faces aglow with wonder.

Her train of thought was distracted by the distant sound of someone tip tapping. She looked around the hall and smiled. There, right in the far corner, was the large figure of Mrs Mould busily rehearsing for her Christmas party performance. Laura's smile deepened as she watched this buxom lady expertly tap dance her way through a complex routine. One thing was certain; this lady had talent in abundance; although, Laura sighed, the same could be said of her weight.

'Miss Windle, I wanted to ask about the Christmas refreshments, the liquid ones I mean,' said a worried voice close by.

Startled Laura looked around to see the tiny figure of Annie standing slightly behind her. As always, Annie had an extremely anxious look plastered across her face – she truly was one of life's great worriers.

'I had thought that this year we might have some sort of cocktail,' Annie continued. She gulped and looked up at Laura, 'I do know that we have enough funds in the catering budget to afford it, plus it might be a bit of a treat for our ladies and...' she cleared her throat then said quickly, 'a bit less boring than just lemonade.'

Laura pursed her lips. 'There is nothing wrong with lemonade Annie. There will also be a measure of good brandy in the Christmas cakes you know, but if you think the ladies would enjoy it...'

'Oh yes, Miss Windle!' Annie blurted eagerly. 'And they do say that Pimms is so very fashionable these days.'

'Pimms?' said Laura. 'I don't quite...'

'It really tastes very like lemonade,' Annie insisted. 'And when you think about it, it's much healthier, 'cause you can put all sorts of fresh fruit and mints in it, so it can't do any harm.'

Laura felt confused at this information. She had always associated lamb chops and garden peas with mint, but if it had become fashionable to put it in some kind of drink then so be it. 'Well Annie,' she said. 'You are quite sure that this is what the other ladies want?'

Annie nodded her head vigorously.

'Then I will see to it.' Laura got out her notebook and wrote, *purchase Pimms for Christmas party*. Then she returned the book to her handbag and watched as Annie darted towards the kitchen to spread the good news. She felt satisfied as she did so – everything in this part of her life was running smoothly. Here at least there was nothing to worry about. She called out a cheerful goodbye as she walked out of the hall, then she began to frown. Now there were other problems to consider; firstly young Penny. Secondly, any more news about Peter, the watchmaker. And thirdly? She gave a deep sigh. Any further news about those dreadful blackmailers?

Chapter Twenty Four

Monday
2pm

Cynthia dashed into her house, tossed her briefcase on the hall table and ran upstairs to get changed.

As she pulled on some slacks and hunted around for a suitable pair of flat shoes, she thought about the events of Saturday night and the woman in the plastic raincoat in light of the surprising information she'd received from Miss Windle yesterday afternoon.

She felt sure she was getting somewhere and that her investigations were moving in the right direction. She was certain that the rain-coated woman of Saturday night was Claire Forbes. She wanted to have a good look at the house in Westdown Road, then if possible, take a very good look at Claire Forbes.

Pulling on a woolly hat she tugged it down over her forehead and tucked in her auburn curls at the back, the last thing she needed was to be recognised. She went downstairs, put on her jacket and picked up her torch, before slipping a small camera and some flash bulbs into her bag – it was best to be prepared for everything. Picking up her shoulder bag she left the house and made her way towards Westdown Road.

As she walked along Cynthia tried to recall the events of Saturday night. What could she remember about the couple? She'd not been able to see the man clearly as he had worn a flat cap. He must have been tall though, for he was taller than the rain coated woman and Cynthia knew that she was a least the same height as herself, even without high heels.

Concentrate on the woman, she told herself, what was it that she remembered about her? The hooded raincoat – it was plastic and had shimmered in a sort of pale green colour, but that could have been caused by the glow of the street lights. She'd only caught the merest glimpse of her face, but she'd noticed her perfume, a sort of over-sweet sickly scent. Cynthia frowned as she tried to place the name of it; it was a well-known brand, but not one she would ever use. As for the woman's make up, Cynthia remembered how the woman had pushed past her and she'd noticed how heavily it had been applied. What else could she recall about her, apart from that and the clacking of her very high heels? The truth was she needed to see the woman in daylight.

As she turned into Westdown Road she slowed her pace and walked past the house for another few hundred yards. Then she stopped and turned around. As she walked towards the house again she looked up at the upstairs windows, there seemed to be none open. The roof looked to be in good condition though and…

Her brain suddenly snapped into high gear when she heard the slam of a house door. A faint smile curved her mouth; her luck was in, she could distinctly hear the sound of high heels click clacking towards the gate. She moved back a few yards, pretended to adjust her shoe lace and waited.

The gate swung open and a hard faced blonde haired woman carrying a shopping bag emerged.

'I was right,' Cynthia murmured, 'this is Claire Forbes.' She watched as, hardly bothering to glance behind her, Claire slammed the gate shut and clattered off in the direction of the High Street. Cynthia followed at a discreet distance.

She watched as the woman came to a halt at the bus stop outside the post office. Cynthia waited and sure enough when the 72 Leeds bus arrived, she saw the blonde woman board it. She felt delighted at this; if the woman was going to Leeds she'd be gone for at least an hour if not more, this would give her plenty of time to have a good look around the house.

Retracing her steps, Cynthia hurried back to Westdown Road. As she reached the gate she stopped and looked at the so-called garden – the usual lawn and flower border had been replaced by a large square of concrete and each corner was adorned with a pink geranium filled vase. Cynthia pulled a face. What a mess! Her own garden was badly in need of sorting out but it was no way near as tasteless as this. Opening the gate she approached the front door and rang the bell. She waited then rang again. No answer. So, no one at home then? Cautiously she made her way towards the back garden. Looking in through the kitchen window she could see a cup and saucer in the sink and a half full bottle of milk on the table. She checked again, only a single cup and saucer? Then it seemed certain there was no-one else in the house.

Feeling more confident, Cynthia ventured further into the back garden, which was overgrown and hadn't been touched in years. Moving on she saw some steps leading down to the green painted back door of the house. She examined it more closely. It was half covered in cobwebs and the paint was starting to peel at the edges. It didn't look as if it had been opened in ages. Treading carefully through the weeds and mud, she went down the steps and gently tested the door. It shuddered slightly but resisted her attempts to open it. She took a backward step and eyed the lock critically. It was very old. Temptation rose in Cynthia's mind. She looked around; should she? If she was caught she would almost definitely be charged with breaking and entering. She pulled open her shoulder bag and brought out a small leather wallet that contained a very special set of keys – a set of keys which legally Cynthia had no right to own. Dismissing her moral voice, and ignoring her years of training, she pulled on her gloves, gave another quick look round and inserted one of the keys into the ancient lock. She jiggled it and finally, with a loud click, the tumblers moved. Giving the door a push, she watched as it creaked slowly open. Peering into the cellar, she allowed her eyes to become accustomed to the darkness. She knew there must be a light switch somewhere but decided against turning it on. The smell of vinegar mingled with the musty scent of potatoes greeted her as she entered. She moved slowly in the direction of the steps upstairs. As she did so she checked out several doors leading to various storage rooms, peering into each one as she passed. Climbing the stairs, she came to the hallway.

She stood for a moment and carefully checked that there was no mud on her shoes before she allowed herself to look around. What a fine old house this was. Remembering Miss Windle's information, her thoughts returned to the offending list. She looked into the living room – a good sized room, but the ultra-modern furniture seemed strangely at odds to the traditional Victorian setting. Crossing the hall she checked out the kitchen and looked in all the drawers one by one, nothing. If such a list still existed it would need to be in a place where no-one would see it. There was nothing in the kitchen, so where was it?

Upstairs seemed the logical answer. She ran up the uncarpeted stairs and checked the attic, where Miss Windle had said were three large cardboard boxes all firmly tied with string. Cynthia looked at them closely, the boxes were dusty and none of the knots had been tampered with. She sighed; there was little point in looking there. Feeling disappointed Cynthia went down the stairs and checked out the bathroom, before moving on to the still unfurnished spare rooms. She wandered along the landing until she reached the master bedroom. Opening the door, she stood on the threshold and gaped open-mouthed.

Thick cream-coloured carpet, embellished with large pink roses covered the floor. Cream built-in wardrobes trimmed with ornate gold edging lined the walls of the room and over by the window stood a large kidney-shaped dressing table, over which five spotlight bulbs were placed.

But the showpiece of this room was the large four-poster bed. It too was adorned in cream lace and trimmed with a hundred tiny, pink ribbons. Cynthia had been in many luxurious bedrooms in her time, and many garish ones too if she was honest, but this? She gazed again at the magnificent four poster. It looked as if it had been lifted straight out of a film star's Hollywood bedroom, the only difference being that it wasn't heart shaped.

Tiptoeing across the carpet she could feel her feet sinking into the deep pile and she worried about her shoes again, hoping she wasn't leaving a trail of mud in her wake. On reaching the head of the four poster bed she stood and looked down at it for a moment. It had a deep frill round the edges and stood high off the floor. Giving in to temptation, she grasped one of the posts then, leaning forward, ran her fingers over the lace covered bedspread – it was luxurious, soft and springy. She felt a twinge of envy, she had always wanted a four poster bed, but Harry had been outraged when she'd suggested it.

'No!' he'd protested, 'I'm not having folk thinking I'm a pimp.'

Her gaze moved on towards the bedside table and again she stared in amazement. Not only was there a telephone on it, but it was a cream coloured telephone. Cynthia glared down at it angrily. She'd been trying for months to get an extension from her house to her office, but British Telecom has stubbornly insisted that there was a waiting list. So then, this woman must have friends in high places.

She opened the bedside table drawers looking for the list, but was met with the same sense of disappointment. Moving on to the fitted wardrobes, she slid the doors open only to find it crammed full of ladies clothes. Crossing the room to the dressing table she searched the drawers. She had almost given up hope when right at the back of the bottom drawer she found a large brown covered folder. Quickly she fished the folder out and on opening it, looked at the sheaf of papers that were in there.

Cynthia had just begun to read it when the bedside telephone rang.

She nearly dropped the folder in surprise. She rushed towards it and reached out to pick up the receiver, then pulled back her hand. She had no right to be here. Just let it ring.

Returning to the window, Cynthia sat on the dressing table stool and started to work her way through the sheaf of papers. She was about two thirds through the documents when she heard a noise that sent shivers down her spine – the sound of a key scraping in the lock downstairs. Her heart thudded. She checked her watch; this couldn't be

Claire, she couldn't have got back from Leeds this early. Then she heard the sound of footsteps on the bare floor boards downstairs. She gulped, they didn't sound at all like ladies shoes. Where could she hide? Closing the dressing table drawer and jumping up, she looked out of the window and felt her anxiety increase. It was high up with no convenient drainpipe nearby.

'Stay calm.' she told herself and crossing the room, slid open the wardrobe doors and tried to squeeze her well-built body inside. But the clothes bounced back and threatened to bring the coat hangers off the rails. 'Don't panic,' she muttered as she pulled the doors closed, 'remember your training.' Where to go? Behind the door? Too risky. Undecided Cynthia hesitated, then from downstairs a male voice called out.

'Claire? You up there?'

Cynthia gulped and looked at the bed. It was the only place left. With her pulse racing she clutched the folder to her chest and scrambled underneath it, pulling the frill down behind her. Breathless, she listened. She could hear footsteps on the stairs. Hugging the folder to her chest, she fought back a growing sense of hysteria. This would be funny if it wasn't so bloody dangerous, she thought. Trying hard to breathe quietly, she listened again. There was the sound of a toilet flushing. Perhaps, as he's answered the call of nature, he might go downstairs again. She started to relax then, without warning...thud... a black shoe landed just near the edge of the frill, closely followed by a grunt and the sudden depression of the bed springs coming to within an inch of her nose.

'Ah!' said a male voice directly above her, 'that's better.' Another thud and the second shoe followed the first.

Now came the smell of sweaty feet. Cynthia wrinkled her nose, turning her head in the opposite direction. Was the man about to take an afternoon nap? If so, she could slide out once he was asleep. Her hopes were dashed when once more the bed springs moved and there came the sound of dialling.

'Hello, that you? Yeah, it's me. I'm over at Claire's place. Just wondered what's happening to the Christmas trees. You got 'em? How much? Okay. Off the back of a lorry, eh? Delivery when? Right, that's good. That'll sort old fancy pants florist.' The man guffawed loudly. 'He had it coming. You want cash...or goods? Goods would be best 'cause there's a bit of a problem with the other side-line. That silly bitch Claire's not helping, she spends money like water. I bet you anything she'll be raiding the shops right now. Yeah, okay mate. Well, I'll see you Thursday then.' There came a click as the receiver was replaced.

Cynthia lay there and thought about the conversation she'd overheard. So was this man the new tenant of that shop on the High Street? If so, why would he want Christmas trees when he must know that Mr Mitchell, the florist opposite him, always sold them? Quick profit, fast turnover was the answer. Must be one of the here today, gone tomorrow crooks that stole trade from hard-working retailers. But was this man connected to the blackmailers? She was sure that Claire Forbes was ties up in it all. She'd been with that man on Saturday night, so she must have known what he was up to. If only she'd stayed a bit longer with Peter she might have got a good look at him. Now all she knew about him was that he was thin, tall and he wore a flat cap.

She lay there hoping for the sound of snoring but all was still. Maybe he doesn't snore? Should she risk it? Inch by inch, she eased her body nearer to the edge. She had just reached the frill when the bedsprings moved. She froze. There came the sound of a match being struck and the scent of sulphur and cigarette smoke. The bedsprings moved again and two feet appeared on the carpet in front of her. She held her breath. Had he heard her moving? No, the feet padded away then returned to the bed after a few seconds.

'How long is he going to be here?' Cynthia thought as she tried unsuccessfully to squint down at her watch. Another thought came into her mind and she froze in horror. What if he's here for the night?

'Think of something else,' she told herself, 'you're not an amateur so stop panicking.' She chewed on her lip and thought about the folder she was still clutching and the list that Miss Windle had mentioned. She had to find it, that was top priority. It could be in the folder, but there had to be more evidence than just one sheet of paper. There must be something else. Cynthia's lips tightened; it was clear that Miss Windle hadn't told her everything. She was almost sure the list was in the folder but when she got home the first thing she'd do would be to contact Miss Windle. She sighed softly. Meanwhile all she could do was lie here and wait...

*

Claire Forbes got off the bus and made her way home. On the whole her little shopping spree had been successful. She'd treated herself to some nice silk panties, some lovely nail polish and a beautiful silk scarf. You could never have too much underwear, she thought as she trotted along, and it was great that she could afford to buy some without worrying about the money, it cheered her up no end. She smiled; besides she wanted to look nice for Lennie.

She wondered how Lennie was getting on with the moving in and stocking of his shop. It seemed to be taking him forever and lately, she'd discovered that he was not as wealthy as she'd thought, which was worrying. 'Either that or he is downright tight-fisted,' she muttered. When she'd first met him he'd seemed such a wonderful man; quite handsome in a skinny sort of way. Smashing car, one of life's... what did they call 'em? Yes that's it, 'tycoon's'.

She frowned as she trotted along; lately she was starting to feel a bit disillusioned with him. He did nothing but moan about money and some of his so-called mates weren't half rough. Also, she was getting the distinct feeling that he was going off her, especially when she did a bit of shopping. Claire felt furious about this, surely he must want her to look nice? So why did he keep complaining? Reaching her front door, she inserted the key and went in.

*

The room was growing darker now and still the man hadn't switched the light on. What time was it? Surely it must be near to half four. Claire had been gone over two hours now. Cynthia's train of thought was distracted by the sound of a key in the lock downstairs, closely followed by the tip tapping of lady's shoes. That had to be Claire returning.

The man on the bed called out 'Claire?'
'Where are you?'
'Up here, where do you think?'
'Hang on a mo, I'm coming,' There came the sound of footsteps on the stairs, a light came on, two beautiful tan high-heeled shoes appeared near the bed fringe and an outraged voice yelled. 'Who sent *you* here? Where's Lennie? And what are you doing on my bed with your mucky clothes on? Why are you using my soap dish as an ashtray? Now you've gone and got fag ash all over me bedspread.'

'Hold on! Hold on! Let me get a word in, will you? Didn't Lennie phone you? He said he would.'

'No, he did not.' Claire shouted, 'and gerrof my lovely bedspread, you're ruining it.'

'It'll wash,' said the man. 'Besides, I took me shoes off. What you been up to? Been buying up Schofields again? Bet them shopkeepers don't half rub their hands with glee when they see you coming?'

'That's none of your business.'

There came the crackle of carrier bags, 'Go on, let's have a look.'

'Gerrof me shopping, and tell me why you're here.'

There came the rustle of silk. 'Cor!' said the man softly. 'That's pretty.'

'Will you get your mucky paws off me smalls?'

'Aren't you going to try them on for me?'

'Like hell I am, just give me them back.' There came the sound of a struggle, a resounding slap and the bedsprings creaked ominously.

'Here!' Claire cried out angrily. 'Get your filthy hands off my bum!'

'Rotten spoilsport,' the man muttered and the bedsprings creaked again. 'You got no sense of fun.'

'Lennie's going to show you some fun when I tell him what you tried to do.'

'As if,' the man sighed. 'Lennie sent me here. He wants you to have a look at some stuff he's getting over at Skipton.'

'Why me? He's never asked me about goods before.'

'How the hell do I know? I'm only the driver... he's buying some ladies stuff and wants a woman's opinion.'

'Alright then, but you behave. Have I got time for a quick cup of tea?'

'Better not, I've been here ages... and you know what Lennie's temper's like.'

'Let's get off then.'

Cynthia heard the sound of high heeled shoes going down the stairs, the feet reappeared at the bed fringe and the shoes were slipped back on.

'Here, wait up.' The man shouted after her, 'I'm coming.' And Cynthia heard the bedroom door close.

She let out a huge sigh of relief, she'd had visions of being stuck here for the night, but she lay still, straining her ears, listening to the movements downstairs. She had to be sure. After a couple of minutes she heard Claire and the man departing and the slam of the door closing behind them. Thank God. At last she was safe.

She wriggled out from under the bed and stretched. Oh what a relief that they'd left the light on. Her first impulse was to head for the safety of her home but then she looked down at the folder and remembered. First, find the list. Next, find the information about the other victims that should be with it.

Searching through the folder she got the list of names but nothing else. It was clear that Claire was no fool; she would have hidden the rest somewhere else in the house. But where? She thought about this. Question: what is the oldest trick in the world when you wanted to hide something? Answer: put it somewhere where it's so visible that it becomes invisible. So, Cynthia told herself, look again. She checked her watch; if Clare and the man were going over to Skipton that could take an hour, but if for some reason Claire had forgotten something, they might return. She could not risk it. She withdrew the list from the folder, photographed it, returned the folder to the drawer then hurried downstairs.

She went into the kitchen and using her torch stood near the doorway looking around. Where could the papers be? She looked in the fridge, the breadbin, but no luck there. Moving to the Welsh dresser she checked the tea and coffee jars but again no success. Time was running out. She was about to give in and try again another day when she brushed against a dark brown vase, almost knocking it off the dresser. She grabbed at it; that would be all she needed, breaking a vase when burgling a house. Putting it back in its place she glanced at the flowers that had fallen out of it, they were pink roses; artificial of course. Shining her torch on the flowers she picked them up and started to put them back in the vase. It was then that she heard a faint crackle. She stared at the flowers for a second, then pulled them out once more. Shining her torch into the vase she could see a folded wad of papers at the bottom. Eureka! Quickly she fished them out, read through them, and photographed the documents. Then, having returned them and the flowers to the vase, she carefully put it back in its rightful place and hurried down into the cellar.

Chapter Twenty Five

Monday
4.30pm

Laura Windle sat in Marilyn Lemming's front room and waited patiently for young Penny-Ann to come home from school. For the second time in the last few minutes she refused Marilyn's offer of a cup of tea and watched as Marilyn stood at the window waiting for her daughter to return.

'Perhaps she's been kept in for detention, Miss Windle,' Marilyn said, 'the school's always doing that.'

Laura nodded politely although she knew that according to Miss Smithson, the headmistress, Penny-Ann hadn't been at school today. The girl had been playing truant, but that was not the reason for her visit.

She was about to speak when Marilyn said, 'She's here now,' and rushed towards the front door.

'Where the hell have you been, young lady? School was over thirty minutes ago,' Laura heard her say. 'Now don't just stand there, there's someone here to see you.'

The door swung open and Penny-Ann came into the room. She looked dirty and untidy.

'Hello, Penny,' Laura smiled. 'Now I do not want to keep you from your tea, I am sure you must be hungry, but I have come to ask for your help...'

'She's not been nicking stuff from the newsagents again, has she?' Marilyn interrupted.

'No!' Laura glared at her. 'Now, if you would allow me to continue?'

'Sorry Miss Windle, but she ain't half a wrong un... 'cause if she's been stealing...'

'She has not been stealing and that is not why I am here.' Laura said icily. She smiled again at the little girl then said quietly. 'Now then Penny-Ann, I wanted to talk to you about something that happened last Friday night.'

Penny-Ann looked at her warily and edged slightly nearer to the door.

'Do not be frightened, no one is going to harm you, but I have been told you did a little errand for someone ...'

''Ere, I was on late shift on Friday. Who you been running errands for?'

'Marilyn!' Miss Windle looked at her sharply.

'Sorry, it's just she gets up to all sorts the minute my back's turned.'

'What can you tell me about this errand, Penny?'

Penny glanced at her mother then at Laura. She said hesitantly, 'There was this fella, see. He said he'd give me a pound if I'd go collect an envelope down at the Bowling Green. So I did 'cause I was hungry and I wanted to get some chips.'

'You could buy a lot of chips for a pound, Penny,' Laura said, 'but can you tell me a bit more about this man?'

'Did he touch you?' interrupted Marilyn anxiously.

'Course not,' Penny said, 'I'm not thick you know.'

'About this man,' Laura continued determinedly. 'What did he look like?'

'Ever so tall and thin... and he had mucky finger nails.' Penny said. 'But he had a nice car, so I thought he must be rich.'

Laura leaned forward. 'Penny, can you remember what kind of car it was? It would have had some letters and numbers on the front and back of it. Can you remember seeing them?'

'It was dark blue, ever so shiny, had a radio too, 'cause I could hear some music playing... but I don't know what kind of car it was and I didn't see no numbers.' She looked at Miss Windle. 'It was dark you see.'

'That's very good, Penny. You have done well. Is there anything else that you can remember about the man?'

'He wore a flat cap and he smelled of smoke. I think he was holding a cigarette.'

'Thank you Penny, that was very observant of you.' Laura repressed a sigh and got to her feet. It was as much as she could glean from Penny without frightening her. If only the girl had got the registration number of the car. As it was all she had was a vague description of a tall man who smoked cigarettes. She smiled and thanked Penny's mother and told her how helpful her daughter had been. She said her goodbye's and had been about to warn Penny about taking money from any strangers, but before she could speak Marilyn interrupted again.

'Don't you dare talk to any fella's ever again. How many times have I told you to come straight home and not hang about on the streets...?'

'I told you... I was hungry.'

Laura had closed the door quietly on Penny's reply and walked out into the street. She had worries enough without being involved in a family row.

Her thoughts returned to Cynthia, she felt relieved now that she had told her about Julia's list, Cynthia had said she would be in touch as soon as she had more news. Meanwhile there was nothing more she could do except wait.

Taking a short cut, she turned into Eastwood road. It ran along the back of the High Street and from this road she could see all the nice gardens, not that there were many flowers about at this time of year but the greenery and shrubs were all so refreshing. She paused as she saw a figure she recognized in Mr Mitchell's garden. She stopped at the gate and called out 'Good afternoon, Mrs Thackeray.'

Edna Thackeray looked up from stacking bits of wood and branches together into a pile and smiled. 'Hello Miss Windle. Out for a walk?'

'Just doing an errand,' Laura said, 'you are busy, I see?'

'Yeah, just going to have a little bonfire whilst the weather's dry. I like to keep things tidy, and it's nice to see a warm blaze on a winter's night.'

That was all very well but she is always making bonfires, Laura thought, she should remember to warn the neighbours to bring their washing in first. 'How is Mr Mitchell?' she asked.

'Oh, he's busy as ever sorting out his flowers,' Edna said as she put a match to the wood pile and tossed a few more bits of wood on to it. She looked across at Miss Windle and said confidingly, 'He's getting steak and kidney pud for his tea tonight.'

'You do spoil him,' Laura said, as she watched Mrs Thackeray add yet more wood to the flames, but then she is a far better lodger than the dreadful Adrian. She felt a sense of pride; she had done well to recommend Mr Mitchell to Mrs Thackeray for lodgings some years ago. Except for the woman's constant liking for bonfires those two seemed to get on well. She shivered and rubbed her hands together and said. 'It's getting colder and I had better get along then before it gets too dark. Please give Mr Mitchell my regards. Have a good evening and enjoy your meal.'

'Will do,' said Mrs Thackeray, 'and you have a good night too, Miss Windle.'

Laura hurried home. She felt so cold, it would be nice to have a good strong cup of tea and something nice and hot for supper, she thought, as she put the key in the lock, but as the door opened the first thing she heard was the telephone ringing.

She hurried down the hall and picked up the receiver. 'Hello?'

'Miss Windle? Cynthia here... about our little search.'

'Oh, were you successful?'

'Yes... but it seems there are more complications. I've found some other documents relating to the list.'

'Oh, of course! Why did I not remember that? That would be the list of the offences that your blackmail victims were guilty of, Cynthia, I am so sorry, I should have thought of that. This is my fault entirely.'

'Not to worry, I've photographed them and I'll get them to the city chemists first thing tomorrow for developing and enlarging.'

'That is wonderful, the things that they can do these days.'

'I was going to suggest that I come along to your house tomorrow and tell you what I overheard whilst at Claire's house. That is, if you're not too busy?'

'You'd be most welcome, this problem must have top priority. We cannot allow innocent villagers to be threatened like this.'

'I'll see you at about six thirty then?'

'That would be fine and thank you for letting me know.'

Laura heard the click as Cynthia rang off. She put down the receiver and wandered into the kitchen. This situation was getting more and more complicated. She should have remembered to tell Cynthia about Julia's letter to Claire and she should have realised that there would be more details about the possible victims than just the names on a list. She made a drink and looked down at her cup of tea. Shivering again she rubbed her arms, was it really the cold or was her blood getting thinner with old age? Reaching a decision she went over to the cupboard, got out a small bottle of brandy and poured a measure of it into her tea. As she drank the tea she felt the warmth seep through her. What was it that Julia used to say when she took a drink or two? *'It's all purely medicinal, Laura.'* She couldn't help but smile as she thought about that remark and her late friend.

'What kind of a tangled web did I weave and where will it ever end?' she thought quietly to herself..

Chapter Twenty Six

*Monday
6.30pm*

It was dark already and bitterly cold, but still no sign of snow. Simon shivered, pulling on his jacket as he went outside to begin dismantling the display of Christmas wreaths and flowers, and bring them indoors for the night.

As he did this, he looked across the street at the lighted window of the newly tenanted shop. He assumed that the tenant was still on the premises and in the process of moving in. But as there was a huge white poster plastered across the window declaring they were 'Opening Soon', it was impossible to see if any goods were on display.

'He'd better get a move on,' Simon muttered, 'otherwise by the time he gets that shop open we'll be well into the New Year.' Not that Simon was bothered about *when* the shop opened, it was what they intended to sell that worried him. The last thing he needed was a cut-price war in the few weeks that remained in the run up to the holidays. That would be dangerous.

He took another long look at the shop opposite before closing and locking the door. Then he strode over to his work bench and checked the Christmas order book. Having reassured himself with the numbers, he smiled in satisfaction and put the book back in the drawer. Nothing to worry about there, plenty of orders for Christmas trees and poinsettias, but he must remember to check on the delivery times.

'Why am I fussing like this?' he asked himself. 'I'm an established florist, well known throughout the village and my customers know that my flowers are good.' Yet still the nagging doubts lingered. 'I'm just not going to think about it anymore,' he announced loudly, and with that he emptied the till, switched off the lights, then sniffing the air appreciatively, murmured, 'Steak and kidney pud tonight, just as Edna promised.' His stomach gave a rumble as he picked up his cash box and headed towards the kitchen.

Edna glanced up and smiled at him as he came through the door, 'Supper's not quite ready yet, Simon, just waiting for the potatoes to be done.'

'Smells great,' he said as he took off his jacket and sat down at the table, 'what's for afters?'

Edna turned from the stove to look at him, 'I thought something light... just a bit of fruit salad, if that's okay?'

'Course it is,' he said. 'Now you sit down for a minute and tell me what you've been up to.' He glanced at the charcoal streaks on her apron.

'Bet you've been out working in the garden again.'

Edna's eyes sparkled as she seated herself. She beamed at him, 'It did need a bit of tidying up, Simon. There were twigs and bits of old wood and rubbish everywhere so I made a little fire.' She leaned across the table and added, 'You see, the thing about fire is it cleanses, just like water.'

Simon nodded in agreement; if, apart from the cooking and cleaning, there was one thing Edna was good at, it was making bonfires. He was sure that the woman had ice in her veins instead of blood, for she always felt the cold.

'Better just drain the potatoes then we'll be ready.' She got up and carried the saucepan to the sink.

Simon loosened his collar and wiped his forehead, that's why it was always so warm in the flat even in summer, she was forever switching the heating on. He could understand it being hot in the kitchen, but whatever the time of year this heat was everywhere, except, of course in the shop. He smiled as he recalled an incident a couple of years back when Edna had first moved in. He'd gone into the shop one winter morning to find two electric heaters going full blast and half of his stock of cut flowers already wilting. He'd had stern words with Edna on that day and from that day onwards, she'd left the shop well alone.

Ten minutes later he pushed away his plate and loosened his belt. 'Thank you, Edna that was very nice as always.'

Edna nodded and began to clear away. Simon stood up and said, 'you sit down a minute. I'll make my coffee... would you like some as well?'

Edna hesitated, 'No thanks,' she said.

She looks uneasy, Simon thought. But then again, she'd been quiet and withdrawn these last few weeks, ever since the blind man had paid her a visit. Who the hell was he? Simon wondered, and why had his visit made Edna suddenly decide that she wanted to move? He sighed; he'd tried to talk to her about her decision. He'd even offered to greatly reduce her rent, for this woman was worth her weight in gold. But no, she'd tightened her lips, stared at the floor and stubbornly insisted that she wanted to go.

When he'd asked for a reason and tried to ask her about the blind man, she'd just run her fingers through her grey hair and scurried away to her room. Now as he watched her clear away the dishes, he tried once more to persuade her to stay. There had to be a reason why she wanted to leave. 'Edna,' he said, 'leave the tidying up a minute and sit down please.'

She looked at him anxiously and obeyed.

He smiled at her. 'There's no need to look so worried. I'm not going to accuse you of running off with the family silver or anything. It's just that I've been thinking about you leaving and I've an offer that might interest you.'

Edna did not reply, she looked down at the tablecloth and began to fold it nervously through her fingers.

'Edna,' he went on, 'we've known each other for quite a while now and I think you'll agree that we get along quite well.'

'It's not that Simon...'

'Will you let me finish? I have to say you've been a wonderful lodger, to say nothing of all the meals and cakes you've made for me...' he broke off and looked down at her, but she still refused to meet his gaze.

'How would it be,' he continued, 'if I were to offer you the job as cook and housekeeper, and the lodging would be rent free? That would solve your money problems.'

'That's not the problem, Simon,' Edna blurted, 'don't you see?' She jumped up and clapping her hand over her mouth, dashed off to her room.

With a deep sigh Simon watched her go. He knew she'd hardly listened to a word he'd said, as if somehow the offer of a job and rent free living was not of the slightest importance. He snorted angrily; if that was not important to a widow at her time of life, then what the hell was? Just what was it that was worrying her?' He stopped in mid thought. No, worrying wasn't the right word – it was more than that. It was as clear as day that Edna was scared stiff about something, but what could it possibly be?

Simon slammed his cup down on the draining board; whatever it was he was determined to find out.

Chapter Twenty Seven

The Farm Boy Inn, Otley.

Martha sat at the corner table in the bar and sipped nervously at her gin and orange. She'd done it again. As always she had managed to arrive too early. She slid a glance at her watch – she still had five more minutes before she could start worrying. Alfredo had said he'd meet her at 7.30, so that's when he would arrive. She pushed away the thoughts of 'what if he stands me up? And what if he can't get the staff to stand in for him?' He'd hardly close his restaurant for her sake. But then, she reassured herself, he would have phoned her. He was not that type of man.

The pub door opened and Alfredo's tall figure came into the bar. He looked around anxiously and his face lit up with a smile when he saw her. Eagerly he strode towards her. She watched as he approached; what a ruggedly handsome man he was. Then she thought, 'why is a man like him still single?'

'Hello! I'm not late am I?'

Martha laughed, 'No, it's not you, it's me that's early.'

'Thank heavens for that.' He looked down at the table. 'Would you like another drink... or something to eat?'

'No thanks, perhaps later.'

She watched him get his drink from the bar then return to sit down opposite her.

'I'm glad that we arranged to meet up again and this time in more comfortable surroundings. Did you enjoy the Chianti?'

Martha smiled, 'I've only had one glass of it so far, but it was lovely. I'm saving the rest for later.'

'Just so long as it doesn't get cold,' Alfredo warned. He raised his glass of beer, 'to us.'

'Good health,' they clinked glasses, then Martha put down her drink and took a deep breath before continuing. 'Alfredo, whilst it is very kind of you to ask me out for a drink like this, there was another good reason why I chose to come.' She hesitated. 'Would you mind if I speak bluntly?'

Alfredo frowned. 'No, but have I offended you in some way? It is true I should not have entered your café so early in the morning, but I thought…'

'That's not it,' Martha interrupted. 'You see, you and I have another problem. We are business rivals.'

'How so?' Alfredo was puzzled. 'Why is that? I do not sell buns or cakes or pies. My food is Italian. That is all I serve.'

'But you do sell morning coffee and teas. You started doing that six months ago. And the thing is I sell morning coffee and tea. Always have done.'

'I see,' he frowned 'So, this morning coffee? Because I sell it, this affects your business?'

'Very much so. It's my main source of income and that, along with my other personal problems, is causing difficulties.'

Alfredo said. 'The reason I opened and starting selling morning coffee on a trial basis is that one or two of my customers asked me to. I did not realize that it was affecting you,' he smiled at her.'I am sure we can come to a mutual arrangement on that.' He reached across the table and touched her hand. 'As for your personal problems, they are private?'

She evaded his gaze, looked down at the table and said. 'Sort of.'

'Someone is hurting you?'

'No... at least not now.'

Alfredo pounced on this remark. 'Then someone *has* been hurting you. Tell me who.'

Instinctively she fingered the scar on her neck. 'It was all a long time ago Alfredo, but now the past has come back to haunt me.'

There was a silence then Alfredo stroked her hand reassuringly and said, 'Something from the past? Memories can be painful.'

Martha eased her hand away and began to toy with the beer mat.

He said, 'If I can help in any way? Maybe if I just sit here and listen?'

Her lips trembled, she sniffed then blurted, 'Not only am I losing business to you, but the truth of it is I'm being blackmailed.'

Alfredo sat back in his chair and stared at the pretty round-faced woman. There was no need to worry about the coffee morning business, they would work something out together. But what interested him greatly was that her last sentence had an all too familiar ring to it.

He said quietly, 'Do you want to tell me more about this blackmailing thing?'

Martha took a deep breath. 'Three years ago, before my divorce, I committed perjury so that my husband wouldn't be sent to jail and I went in his place.'

'What man would do this? Knowingly send his wife to jail for a crime that he committed?'

'I had thought it was all over and done with, but now…'

Alfredo grasped her hands. 'Martha, this should not be happening.'

She looked at him, 'I know but let me explain. My ex-husband, Bert, was involved in a serious motorway accident, he'd been drinking heavily and shouldn't have been driving. He knew that if he admitted that he was at the wheel, he would go to prison and lose his job. So he made me say that I was the driver.'

'How could he do such a thing to his wife?'

Martha sighed, 'He could and he did, and even though I paid the price, I'm still being blackmailed. I've already paid two instalments, so I decided to employ a private investigator.'

'Cynthia Roberts?'

'You know her?'

'Martha., there is something I must tell you, though I know this is no consolation. Yes I know Cynthia Roberts because … I too have need of her services.'

She stared at him. 'Not you as well? Being blackmailed, I mean.'

He nodded, 'and, like you, it all happened years ago.'

'Do you want to talk about it?'

Alfredo gave a grim smile. 'To be brief it was all to do with my greed and the use of mushrooms. Like you I thought I had paid the price, but it would seem someone else has other ideas.'

'What are you going to do?'

'I have been told I have to leave a payment at the cemetery at 7pm on the Sunday after this one, but I think I may have other plans.' He smiled at her, 'but before that happens, I think we need to come to a mutual arrangement.'

Martha smiled in relief. 'About the morning beverages in your restaurant you mean?'

'Of course!' Alfredo raised his beer glass in salute. 'To harmony, united we stand.' They clinked their glasses together.

'And divided we fall,' agreed Martha.

Chapter Twenty Eight

Wednesday
7.15pm

Cynthia peered into the mirror, applied her lipstick carefully, then checked the result. 'Not too bad for a hard working widow in her forties,' she murmured as she blotted her lips and looked at her reflection. She gave her auburn curls a final fluff then got up, went to her wardrobe and brought out her coat. Having slipped it on she looked down at her feet and sighed; she really hated having to wear high heels except in the office, but she felt that tonight she should make the effort to look smart for Neill. She hadn't seen him for over a year now and it just wouldn't do for a former business friend to think of her as dowdy.

She looked in the shoe drawer for some smart but comfortable shoes and slipped them on. As she went downstairs she wondered whether she should take the car and drive down to the George & Mary, but Otley Road was only a ten minute walk away and after being in the office all day she really needed the exercise. She checked her watch as she went out of the door – it was 7.20. She should get there by 7.30 she thought; unlike most women she liked to be punctual.

*

Neill was already seated at a table with a glass of beer in front of him when she arrived. As soon as he saw her, he jumped up and waved cheerfully. Cynthia grinned as she hurried over to him.

'Did you think I'd not recognise you?' she laughed, as she seated herself opposite him.

Neill beamed at her, 'My dear, I've aged a thousand years since I last saw you, what with all the hard work that I do.' He paused and looked at her critically, 'But as for you? I see in your case time has stood still.'

'You can cut the flattery Neill, you don't fool me.'

'Well, it was worth a try,' Neill grinned. 'I've got to keep practising my social skills with the ladies. Seriously though Cynth, you're looking really well. Now first things first, what would you like to drink?'

Having requested her drink Cynthia sat back and watched Neill as he walked towards the bar. She felt a sense of excitement and a quickening of her pulse as she looked at him. He was without doubt an attractive man, but it was far too soon to be attracted to other men, wasn't it? She thought about her Harry, she still loved him didn't she? She would always love Harry. But he was gone. Even so, this shouldn't be happening, it felt wrong somehow.'

'I'll say it again' Neill said as he stood at the table with her drink. 'Would you like to order some food? I did ask you before but you were day dreaming. They've got a limited menu here, although the Ploughman's lunch seems to be a popular choice, even though it's now evening.' He looked at her, 'we could move on elsewhere and get a proper meal?

Cynthia shook her head, 'No thanks, a sandwich will do, but not just yet, perhaps later. She watched him as he sat down again; a few more strands of grey in his brown hair, which was already thinning. A few more lines around those pale blue eyes and the mouth. To all intents and purposes Neill was a genial man; affable and welcoming and forever joking. Yet she knew from past experience that this was an analytical man, who, in spite of his friendly attitude, had a razor sharp mind.

'Oi!'

She started as she heard the sharp click of his fingers and she looked across at him.

'You were miles away again Cynth,' he said in mock indignation. 'Am I boring you, has it been a long hard day or something?'

Cynthia shook her head, 'So sorry Neill, it's just ongoing case problems that keep sneaking back into my mind.' She took a sip from her drink, leaned forward and said, 'It's so good to see you again, tell me all about what you've been up to.'

'You first,' said Neill. 'How is the new business going? Got plenty of clients? More importantly, are they all prompt payers? Oh, and I forgot to ask, how's your better half by the way? What does he think about you starting up on your...?' He stopped short and stared at her. 'What's wrong Cynth? Have I said something I shouldn't?'

At Neill's mention of the words "your better half", Cynthia felt the blood drain from her face. Hadn't her old bosses told Neill about Harry? They should have done, they were at Harry's funeral after all.

'Cynth! You've gone deathly white. What's wrong?'

'Didn't you know about Harry?'

'He's ill?'

She said quietly, 'He died, Neill. A heart attack, just under a year ago.'

Neill jumped up and put his arms around her. 'Cynth,' he said softly, 'I'm so so sorry. No one told me. Harry is, was, such a nice man, so sensible and straight forward, I liked him so much, you know you have my heart-felt condolences.'

Cynthia swallowed hard, blinked back her tears, then sat up straight and said firmly. 'I'm doing what Harry wanted me to do,' she smiled as she remembered, 'although Harry never believed that I should work for nothing.'

'I agree with that wholeheartedly,' Neill said as he returned to his seat, 'but how are you coping? As I recall you have no immediate family, it must be tough.'

She said sharply. 'Work helps me through it.' She did not want Neill to see how close to tears she was. She needed to be tougher than that. She took another sip from her glass. 'So,' she said, 'enough about me, what about you? What brings you here to Fawdon?'

'Okay then. What can I tell you? Firstly what I will tell you is in the strictest confidence. Also it's because I know I can trust you. My case goes back four years when my company received a claim for fire damage to a house. The claimant in question stated that the whole house was burned down; not only that, the claimant's husband was trapped in the fire and died.' Neill sighed, 'A very sad case indeed and naturally we honoured the claim. The widow told us she was moving away from Leeds and going to live in Harrogate. She led us to believe she was going to live with her sister and so we assumed everything was settled. That was until recently when my company received an anonymous phone call, followed by a letter from a third party. Since then we've received two more letters advising us to reopen the case. The fire, or so the third party claims, was by no means accidental, nor was the death of the claimant's husband. Also when we re-examined the case, the forwarding address that the claimant gave us did not exist. We can find no trace of any siblings of the claimant either. It is now clear she was an only child.'

'Oh, my God!' Cynthia blurted, 'you think it was murder?'

'We just don't know Cynth. All we know is there was a fire and that the claimant's husband was found dead in the ruins of it. And that's why the information I've been given is bringing me to Fawdon.'

Cynthia searched her memory, 'It certainly isn't one of my clients.'

'But you know this village Cynth. Can you think of any recent arrivals to Fawdon in the past few years? This lady would be well into her sixties and comfortably well off.'

'Neill, I honestly can't think of anyone that fits that age group at the moment, what you have to remember is that I only moved back into Fawdon six months ago. We lived out in Shadwell until... well, you know.' She hesitated as, without warning, Miss Windle snapped into her mind and she remembered the conversation that she'd had with her on Monday evening. 'I think I might know someone who may be able to help.'

'Anything at all would help. I'm looking at a time factor of one to three years maximum.'

'I'll talk to the lady in question. I'm sure she'll be eager to help you. In fact we can arrange a meeting with her.'

'That would be great, just tell me when and where.'

'I'll call her and arrange something first thing tomorrow, and now it's my turn to ask you for some advice.' Cynthia smiled, 'I'm dealing with several cases of blackmail in Fawdon and I think I've identified the woman blackmailer, but I need to find out more about the man she's working with. If I give you some details could you use your connections and your vast experience to find out some more for me?'

'Now who's doing the flattering?'

Cynthia's smile deepened into a grin. 'Oh Neill, the whole world knows how clever you are.'

'With words like that how can I refuse. Just give me the details and I'll see what I can find out.' He reached over and squeezed her hand before picking up the menu card. 'Now to the important things in life, I'm sure you must be starving, so what kind of sandwich do you want?'

*

10pm

Cynthia waved goodbye as Neill's car disappeared down the road and then made her way down the path to her front door. She felt relaxed and happy knowing that Neill would do all that he could to help her. Her thoughts turned to the retiree that Neill had mentioned; first thing tomorrow she would phone Miss Windle and ask for her help. All in all she thought, as she put her key in the lock, Neill hadn't changed a bit. He'd got a bit older, but then so had she. She'd thought of asking about his personal life, she knew he'd gone through a difficult divorce some years ago but as to whether he'd found a new love in his life, she was none the wiser.

The front door swung open and she strode through the darkened hall into the kitchen and switched on the light. Then she saw it!

There on the table was a large notice, propped up against the salt and pepper mills. On a stark piece of white card, bright red letters warned:

Mind your own business or else!

Cynthia's heart thumped. Who had been in here? In her house!

She spun around, her eyes searching the room. Nothing had been moved, everything was in its usual place so it couldn't be vandals. How had they got in? She ran back to the front door and, grabbing a torch from the hall stand, examined the lock. Apart from a slight scratch which might have been there earlier, the lock was undamaged. She turned round and ran down the hall to check the back door, but she could see no signs of a forced entry. She frowned; tomorrow she would have to call the locksmith. For a while she stood undecided at the foot of the stairs, then taking a deep breath, went up them. She quickly checked the bathroom and the spare room; everything was as she had left it. Then when she entered her bedroom she stood stock still, for there, pinned to her pillow, was another notice, printed in the same blood red ink.

Keep your nose out or there'll be trouble.

For a long time she stood staring at the message. At first she had felt fear, but now there was no mistaking the burning fire of anger building up inside of her. She strode up to the notice and tore it from the pillow. 'You're not going to get away with this,' she muttered.

She was about to tear the paper into shreds when she hesitated, it could come in useful; so she slipped it in her pocket, marched downstairs and picked up the phone.

Chapter Twenty Nine

Saturday Morning

Peter Greystone lifted the glass lid of the jewellery showcase and rearranged the sparkling bracelets and brooches within. His hand moved carefully, albeit a little shakily, as he placed the items so that the price tags were clearly yet discreetly shown.

Having done this, he closed the lid and stood back to check that everything was well displayed before he returned to his workbench at the rear of the shop.

As he sat down he instinctively touched the dressing on the side of his head. He still It was most embarrassing when customers, on seeing the dressing, asked him what he'd been up to. He'd fobbed them off with a tale about stumbling on the pavement outside, but that excuse had not satisfied Helen, his wife. She really could be a stubborn woman at times.

He recalled how on Saturday night when he'd finally got home, she had stood there and loudly accused him of having a mistress because he was so late. Peter gave a whimsical grin as he reflected on this; what a preposterous idea, as if he had actually found himself a lover who enjoyed beating him up. He had tried to reason with Helen and then he'd realized that nothing but the truth would do. At first she had not believed him, but then he'd been forced to show her the letter. Then came the hysterics and the panicking. What about her? What about the girls? How could they possibly live here if this came out? Helen had been adamant that they would have to move out of the area.

Peter had tried his best to reassure his wife, telling her that the situation was being dealt with, that he'd employed a private investigator, but it was no good. His frown deepened, on Monday night he had watched Helen avidly searching the 'Houses for Sale' column in the Yorkshire Evening Post. He'd decided there was no point in arguing further, the best thing to do would be to let her carry on looking at houses. He just hoped that Cynthia Roberts would find the blackmailer soon. She had said on Saturday night that she needed to check things out further, as she suspected that a man and a woman were working together as a team.

As for the bloke who had attacked him? Peter glanced down at the shelf below the workbench and stroked the knuckle duster thoughtfully. He just wished he'd get one more chance to have another go at the man. The frustrating thing was that all he knew about his attacker was that he was tall and thin and smelled of cigarette smoke…and, importantly, that he was left handed.

The shop doorbell buzzed as a customer came in and he got up to greet her. This morning had been quite busy; in fact, business had been exceptionally good this month. The takings were up even on last year's pre-Christmas figures. This fact made him feel a bit better. He dismissed all thoughts of the blackmailers and gave a friendly smile as he approached his customer, 'Good morning, madam,' he said, 'how may I help you?'

Chapter Thirty

Saturday afternoon

Laura Windle came out of her house, checked that she had locked the door and hurried down to her garden gate. As she reached it she hesitated again and turned to look back at the house. Had she turned the gas off? It had been such a hectic morning, so much so that her mind was buzzing and she was in danger of forgetting something important.

Cynthia Roberts had rung her first thing this morning and invited her to her house for dinner tonight; she had said there was someone that she would like her to meet. Then Cynthia had mentioned something about retirees who had moved into Fawdon recently; it had all sounded very mysterious, and Laura felt puzzled. Still, she reassured herself, perhaps it would all be explained to her later.

Immediately following Cynthia's call, there had been several phone calls from little Annie whom she had placed in charge of the catering and the refreshments for today's Christmas party for the Mother's Union. Laura frowned as she thought about it. Judging from Annie's increasingly anxious tones, things at the church hall were not going well. Annie had gabbled on about there being something of a problem with the liquid refreshments.

When she had listened to Annie complaints Laura reached a decision; she would go along to the church hall and sort things out for herself. She clicked her tongue in annoyance as she turned off the High Street and into Green Lane. So many worrying things were happening all at once. Was Julia's younger sister, Claire, really involved in blackmailing people? How could she be so greedy, after all, she had inherited Julia's house so she should not have any financial difficulties. Her thoughts moved on to Peter Greystone, the watchmaker, and her agitation increased. The poor little man was being threatened by a vicious blackmailer; she had wanted to call in at his shop to see if he was all right, but then there was Annie and the all-important Christmas party to attend to.

'Surely it is not too difficult to arrange a Christmas party,' she muttered angrily as she marched along, 'I have done it for years.' And at the time Annie had been only too keen to do the job. Still, she thought, mistakes can be made. She had always taught the children that they should learn from their mistakes, although some of them never did.

As she approached the Church hall she could hear music and, if she was not mistaken, she was sure she could hear Bing Crosby singing. Her mood lightened, 'White Christmas,' was such a lovely song. She began to relax, surely whatever was worrying Annie could be put right. She walked calmly into the Church hall then stared in amazement at the scene before her.

Several of the mothers were dancing in the hall in a sort of dreamy slow waltz. They seemed to be weaving about unsteadily, giggling and tripping over their own feet. But before she could say a word, the tiny figure of Annie rushed to meet her, her face taut with anxiety.

'I'm so glad you got here Miss Windle,' she gushed. She looked around at the dancing women, 'I just didn't know what to do.'

'What are you talking about?' demanded Laura.

'It's the punch y'see. I never thought, well it never occurred to me that...'

'That what?'

Annie grabbed Laura's sleeve and towed her towards the beverage table. 'You remember when I asked you if you could buy a bottle of Pimms for the party?'

'I remember it well. I bought it and gave it to you three days ago. You told me it was the 'in' party drink,' Laura said.

'I also said it needed lots of fruit and it tasted like lemonade,' Annie replied. She stared down at the near empty punch bowl. 'Only,' she turned to look at the waltzing women, 'they actually thought it was lemonade.' Reaching under the table she brought up a large empty bottle of gin, 'and some bright spark tipped this into it, just to liven things up.' Annie looked up at Laura, her face tight with worry. 'I tried to stop them drinking it, Miss Windle, but every time I turned my back they were pouring themselves another glass.'

'Then this punch is really potent?'

'You're telling me it is. Just look around.'

Uneasily, Laura gazed around the room. Some women were still trying to dance, whilst in the corner of the room, two elderly ladies seated there were already fast asleep. 'Shouldn't we just remove it?' She reached for the punch bowl but before she could pick it up a voice yelled out.

'Oi! Leave that where it is.'

Laura turned to see the large figure of Mrs Mould weaving her way unsteadily towards her.

'Oh Lord,' whispered Annie. She clutched Laura's sleeve tightly. 'She's had three glassfuls already, says it gives her Dutch courage for when she does her rehearsals.'

A warning light went on in Laura's mind. She was well aware of Mrs Mould's weakness for a glass or three of sherry. She gestured to Annie to remove the punch bowl then turned to face Mrs Mould. 'Hello my dear,' she said brightly, 'enjoying the party are we?'

Mrs Mould eyed her warily. 'I am. Don't know 'bout you though.' She swayed unsteadily as she peered at Laura. 'I've just been and got me record and I'm going to play it when Bing's finished.'

Laura cleared her throat, 'Er... wouldn't you like to sit down for a minute?'

'Would I hell as like, not when there's work to be done. I has to do me practising for the pensioners' cabaret y'see. The Vicar says he wants me to do a tap dance for them.' She wrinkled her nose. 'But I reckon that's a bit tame, a bit too prim-like?'

'No, not at all, Mrs Mould. I saw you rehearsing the other day and I thought it was marvellous.'

'Nah.' The music stopped and Mrs Mould brushed past her and put her record on the gramophone. Then she staggered down the hall close to where the window cleaner was working and started to drag some tables together.

Laura began to feel nervous. She followed her. 'What are you trying to do?' she asked.

'I'm going to show you... and them,' she gestured at the dancing women, 'what real dancers do. 'Cause I was a pro in my time y'know and I can still do a bit better than tap dancing, just you wait.' For a second she stood patiently until the new music commenced. Then she removed her shoes and clambered up on to the tables.

'Mrs Mould! Come down this minute!'

'Aw shurrup!' Mrs Mould looked down at Laura. 'You must know this tune? ' She started to sing loudly, 'I can-can, and you can-can, so why should not we two can-can?' With that she began to high kick and by doing so revealed a pair of shocking pink knickers. At this Charlie, the window cleaner, having watched Mrs Mould's earlier antics with interest, caught sight of her bloomers and dropped his bucket to gape open-mouthed.

'Come on Miss Windle,' urged Mrs Mould breathlessly. 'Join in! You must know the "Can-can?"

'If you mean "Orpheus in the Underworld," yes, I certainly do.' Laura said sharply. 'But I did not associate it with a dance routine. Now will you get down?'

'Oh, do give over,' Mrs Mould puffed. 'You were young once, even if it was yonks ago. Everybody in the Universe knows the Can-can. As for its real title? Well, sod that! One kick, two kicks,' she sang breathlessly, 'simple when you know the trick. Turn round, bend down...' With that she turned and, lifting her skirts even higher, presented Laura with a view of her shocking pink posterior.

Laura gasped in outrage and reaching up was on the point of dragging Mrs Mould from the tables when she heard an ominous creaking. She looked at the tables and took a backward step. She shouted, 'please, Mrs Mould! I beg you, get down!' But it was too late. There came an almighty crash as the tables collapsed under the dancing figure who slithered ungracefully to the floor.

Laura rushed to help her. 'Are you alright?'

Mrs Mould looked up at her blearily, 'I reckon I've got a splinter in me bum.' There came an ear piercing screech as the music stopped abruptly.

'Great heavens,' boomed the voice of the vicar as he strode towards them. 'What on earth is going on in here?'

Chapter Thirty One

Laura and Charlie, the window cleaner, helped Mrs Mould to her feet whilst Laura watched open-mouthed as the vicar marched straight into the church hall office. Following as quickly as they could, they went into the office and eased her gently into a nearby chair.

The vicar turned to glare at them, then reached for the phone. 'What's your husband's phone number, Mrs Mould?' he demanded.

Mrs Mould sniffed, 'He'll be at work now Vicar, there's no need to bother him. I'll be alright in a minute or two. I can make me own way home.'

'I could go with her,' Laura volunteered.

'You'll do no such thing, Miss Windle,' the Vicar replied. 'I will not tolerate members of my parish behaving in such a drunken, disorderly manner and in broad daylight too.' He glared again at the culprit. 'Now, Mrs Mould, your husband's phone number, if you please!'

Laura watched tight lipped as the vicar dialled the number Mrs Mould had given him. She found it hard to control her anger. What a pompous man he was. Had he no sense of compassion, no understanding of human weakness? After all, this was a Christmas party. It was at such times that people did over indulge. She felt someone nudge her arm and turned to see Charlie still standing beside her.

'Alright if I clear off now, Miss Windle?' he whispered.

Laura nodded. 'Yes, thank you for your help, Charlie.' She watched him move silently out of the office, then she gave an inward sigh as the Vicar's voice reached her again.

'Mr Mould? So sorry to have to phone you at your work place. Yes, it's Reverend George Wilson speaking. The reason I am calling you is about your wife, Mrs Mould. She is I'm, um... rather unwell. No, no, she is not in hospital or anything, but she did have a slight accident and I have to say as a result of this some of my church tables have been damaged.'

The vicar paused and held the phone away from his ear as shouts of outrage came from the receiver. Mrs Mould groaned and put her head in her hands.

'Mr Mould,' the vicar interrupted loudly, 'I feel sure we can deal with the repayments for the tables at a later date, but in the meantime it would be most helpful if you could come and collect your wife in your car.' He turned to look at Mrs Mould critically, 'As she seems to be... rather unsteady. She'll be waiting at the church hall office. Thank you.' He replaced the receiver, looked at Mrs Mould, and said, 'Your husband will come to collect you in a few minutes.'

'Oh my Lord!' Mrs Mould groaned as she buried her face in her hankie.

'I could just as easily have escorted her home,' Laura blurted.

'There really was no need for all this fuss and now you've called Mr Mould away from his work.'

'I ain't half gonna cop it when he gets here,' sobbed Mrs Mould. 'He's gonna be blazing mad, you'll see.' She rubbed at her eyes again.

'I did what had to be done.' The vicar said righteously. 'I cannot have drunken women cavorting around in my church hall and on the streets of Fawdon.'

'She was not all that bad,' Laura protested loudly.

'I do not intend to argue with you, Miss Windle.' Suffice it to say that this woman was behaving in an unseemly manner and caused considerable damage to church property.'

'As for the damage to the tables, I can assure you, Reverend Wilson, it will be paid for,' Laura insisted.

'Then I will leave this matter in your more than capable hands, Miss Windle. I have more important work to do. Good day to you both.' With that he marched out of the door.

Then why did he not leave it to me in the first place, instead of behaving so self-righteously? Laura wondered. She looked down at the red eyed face of Mrs Mould and placed a reassuring hand on her shoulder. 'I will stay with you until your husband arrives,' she said gently. She thought about the impending arrival of the man, better known in the village as the local 'Scrooge,' a man known for his meanness, who disapproved of just about any entertainment whatever; except...' a distant memory stirred in Laura's mind.

'I'll get the money for the tables as soon as I can, Miss Windle,' Mrs Mould said anxiously.

'I will need to get an estimate first, so try not to worry.' Laura broke off as she heard the slam of a car door and footsteps approaching.

'That'll be him now,' groaned Mrs Mould. 'You go on home if you like. I'll deal with my Desmond. Lord knows I've had enough practice.'

Laura's jaw tightened. 'I will stay here with you...' she broke off again as a tall round-shouldered man pushed straight past her and stood glaring down at Mrs Mould.

'What the hell have you been up to now, you stupid bitch?' He shouted.

'It is not all that serious, Mr Mould,' Laura intervened. 'Just a little too much of the festive spirit.'

'You've been at the booze again. Can't you leave it, you big fat lump.'

'Mr Mould! There really is no need for insults.'

'She's my wife isn't she? I can say what I like.' He stared hard at Laura before continuing. 'Here's me trying to live a decent life avoiding all of life's temptations – cigarettes, drinking, card playing and other such wicked things – and here she is back on the bottle every time me back's turned. What will people think of me, eh? Why can't she be like me, eh? Sober and hard working.'

'Are you so perfect then?' Laura said icily.

'I'm an honest man,' Mr Mould replied.

'That was not my question,' Laura said. 'Do you then have no faults, no weaknesses?' Laura thought about the photo she still had of Mr Mould. It had been taken more than two years ago and it was not so much the picture of Mr Mould, but the picture of the premises he had been about to enter at that time that was of particular interest. Laura hesitated and decided to probe further. 'Do you not believe in such a thing as lady luck? Or the element of chance? Do you *never ever* take chances?'

Mr Mould stared suspiciously at Laura and his face turned pale. 'What are you getting at?'

'I am sure if you think about it you will know the answer to that. It might be a good idea to look at your own faults rather than constantly criticizing your wife's weaknesses.'

'You just mind your own business.' Mr Mould muttered weakly. He leaned over his wife and quickly pulled her to her feet. 'Let's get you home,' he said and guided her to the door.

'It would help if you were to find out *why* your wife is drinking,' Laura called after him. 'But I am sure you know the answer to that as well.'

Laura stood and listened to the sound of a car door slamming and driving off. She wondered whether she should have told Mr Mould about the photo she had taken of him two years ago as he entered the betting shop. No, she decided, she would only play that last card if Mrs Mould's situation got worse.

She took a deep breath and checked her watch. Good heavens it was close to four o'clock already and she had so much to do. Feeling angry and frustrated, she made her way home.

Chapter Thirty Two

Saturday

Having phoned Alfredo from her office and brought him up to date with the blackmail situation, Cynthia decided to take the rest of the afternoon off and she arrived home just after lunch. She fought back her sense of guilt for leaving early and justified it with the thought that she needed to buy some food for her guests, as it had been a long time since she'd invited guests to dinner; a very long time.

It was not that she wanted to impress anyone, but Miss Windle had been very helpful during these last few weeks and she thought that this would be a good way of showing her appreciation.

Opening her shopping bag, she took out the joint of beef and some fruit and vegetables that she had bought on the way home and looked at them critically; it should be more than enough for three people. She prepared the beef and put it in the oven to roast slowly. Having done this she stood for a while trying to decide what to make for dessert. Her Harry had always loved fruit salad, but she felt she should make something more traditional for Miss Windle. She looked down at the apples that she'd placed on the kitchen table – they would be perfect for an apple pie. Yes, that would do nicely, she was sure it would suit everyone.

Most importantly, Neill would be coming as well. She was looking forward to seeing him again. He really had been reassuring last night when she'd phoned him and told him about the messages in her home. Neill had driven straight back from Leeds and checked out each room again with her. Then he had recommended that because of her profession she was at risk and she should have a burglar alarm installed. He'd pointed out that although changing the lock might be good, if this had been a professional burglar, as he suspected, then putting a different lock on the door would be unlikely to make a difference.

Neill had also touched lightly on the subject of informing the police.

Cynthia thought about this, but as nothing had been taken she decided against it. Besides, she had her own suspicions as to who the intruder might be. She looked at the clock, the locksmith would be coming round in a couple of hours and she could shop around for quotes on burglar alarms next week. Neill had also suggested that she should think about getting a dog. The main objective of this being to raise the alarm, a dog barking would act as a deterrent for the modern day burglars who could break in anywhere. Cynthia had smiled when she thought about that, it would be something she would have to consider in the future. She glanced at the clock again, she had better get a move on. She went to the larder and got out the ingredients to make the apple pie.

It was no good worrying about last night's incident, she told herself as she peeled the apples, there was work to be done.

*

Saturday
7pm

Laura Windle smiled politely at Cynthia's request and seated herself at the dining room table. She was still angry after the events of this afternoon and she felt sorry for poor Mrs Mould, but she was sure that she had dealt with the situation as best she could. Perhaps, one day, Mr Mould might learn from what she had said? Although she had the distinct feeling that in Mr Mould's case, her words had fallen on stony ground.

Stop it! Concentrate on the now, Laura told herself. You are a guest in Cynthia's home and you must behave appropriately. She looked around and as she did so, her sharp eyes took in every detail of the comfortably furnished room. She nodded in appreciation; it was tastefully, if a little too brightly, decorated, but then this was very much Cynthia Roberts' style. She risked another glance at the gentleman seated next to her. He was quite a handsome fellow, slightly rugged in appearance but with a charming smile and an easy going manner and within minutes, he had put her at her ease.

Cynthia had introduced them earlier of course. Apparently he was a former business acquaintance of hers, Neill Collinson was his name.

Looking down at the table she inspected the cutlery with a critical eye – not solid silver, but definitely top quality Sheffield plate. She smiled in silent approval as she allowed her fingers to gently smooth the Irish linen tablecloth. As for the wine glasses, now they were definitely Waterford crystal. She felt pleasantly surprised, for in spite of Cynthia's dark past, she certainly knew about the finer things in life. Still, Laura remembered, Harry Roberts, Cynthia's late husband, had been a successful businessman and it was logical that Cynthia would have had to entertain many of his clients.

'Hope you like vegetable soup, Miss Windle? Cynthia said as she placed the bowl in front of her. 'Although I must admit that it's of the tinned variety, I just hadn't the time to make some fresh.'

Startled Laura looked up at her, 'I'm sure it will be splendid, my dear.' She sipped a small spoonful. 'Yes indeed, very tasty.' She looked across at Neill and said, 'It is so pleasant to see a new face here in Fawdon, Mr Collinson, were you thinking of moving here?'

'Please call me Neill,' he replied, 'and no, I live on the other side of Leeds.'

'Neill's an insurance investigator,' Cynthia said, 'and his speciality is arson investigations and fraud.'

'I'm sort of self-employed,' Neill explained. 'Most of the big insurance companies employ me on a contract basis.'

'He's very good at his job,' Cynthia remarked. She grinned at him, 'He seems to have quite a knack for flushing out pyromaniacs.'

Laura's interest deepened. 'Indeed,' she said, 'how remarkable.' She looked across at Cynthia. 'I must say that although we've had the occasional fire here in Fawdon, and very distressing they were as well, as far as I know we have not had any pyromaniacs here in the village.' she thought for a moment, 'Saying that, I could name quite a few shoplifters that live in the area and we have petty thieves in abundance.'

'Well I'm relieved to hear that, Miss Windle,' Neill smiled, 'although I've got plenty of work as it is.'

'The reason he's here, Miss Windle,' Cynthia interrupted, 'is that he's come to ask for help. Neill is trying to find a certain lady.' She hesitated and looked from Neill to Miss Windle. 'And I thought that you would be the best person to advise him. After all you do know just about all the senior citizens in Fawdon.'

Laura cleared her throat. 'Well, no, not quite, my dear. There are also quite a few recluses that live here and they can be very unsociable, if you know what I mean?'

'Miss Windle,' Neill said. 'I would ask that you treat the information that I am about to give you as strictly confidential.' He looked at Cynthia. 'Cynthia has assured me that you can be trusted, so I will tell you the person I am looking for will be well into her sixties and comfortably well off. As far as we know, she would have moved to

Fawdon about two years ago. The reason I am trying to identify the lady is that she is strongly suspected of arson and perhaps, worse.'

Laura stared at him. 'Worse? Good Gracious! I dare not ask what that might mean.'

Neill smiled and touched her hand. 'Then let us first deal with the arson, providing we can find the person concerned.'

Laura looked from Cynthia to Neill, 'I will of course treat all that I have heard with the strictest confidence. You both have my word on that. As for finding this lady, I will do all that I can to help.'

Cynthia smiled at her, 'I hope we're not asking too much of you, Miss Windle, you've already been more than helpful with my blackmail cases.'

'Do you know who the blackmailers are?' Neill asked.

'After Monday afternoon's visit to Claire's Forbes' house, I'm certain that she is one of them.' Cynthia said.

Laura nodded, 'I have to agree with you, although it is with some reluctance, as she is my late friend's baby sister. She is also a newcomer to the village.'

'Does she have a boyfriend?' Cynthia asked. 'Only from what I overheard on Monday afternoon the man and Claire kept referring to someone called Lennie.' She frowned. 'Yes, I'm almost sure Lennie was the name, although it might have been Bennie. Anyway, what was also interesting was that the man lying on the bed took a phone call and from what I could makeout, they had bought some Christmas trees that had supposedly 'fallen off a lorry' and they were going to 'sort old Fancy pants' the florist out.'

'By that would they mean Mr Mitchell?' Laura interrupted. 'He is our only florist.'

'Agreed,' Cynthia said. 'But who are they?'

'Not that I want to jump to conclusions,' Laura replied, 'but the only new business on the High Street is the empty shop, which, I happened to notice, has recently been taken over.' She leaned forward and said confidingly. 'Rumour has it the tenants are going to sell 'fancy goods', whatever that might mean.'

'It could mean anything Miss Windle.' Neill said. 'These days traders can sell almost anything that they like, now that trade restrictions have been lifted.'

Cynthia looked at Neill. 'Do you believe in coincidences?'

'I believe in checking everything. So where did Clare Forbes live before she came here? Perhaps she's brought her boyfriend with her.'

'She's not from Leeds. Miss Windle has given me her old address and that's in Sheffield...' She broke off. 'Now what are you smiling at?'

'Just that I'll be working over in Manchester and Sheffield on Monday, so if you give me the address, I'll see what I can find out.'

'It would seem that the way is being made clear.' Laura murmured.

'Or that for once we got lucky,' Cynthia said. She stood up and began clearing away the soup plates. 'Enough of the shop talk, let's enjoy our meal.' She smiled down at them. 'I do hope you both like roast beef?'

*

9.45pm

Laura put her key in the door and turned to wave goodbye to Mr Collinson. Then she closed and bolted the door, wandered into the living room and sank down gratefully into the armchair. It had been such a frantic day and she was starting to feel bewildered by it all. After a few minutes she sat up straight and shook her head roughly from side to side. 'This will not do,' she told herself sharply, 'you have to organize your thoughts. So then,' she murmured, 'first things first.' Now, it was likely that as well as blackmailers they had an arsonist living in the village, as if things were not bad enough already.

What was happening to Fawdon? It used to be such a quiet, friendly village, but now? Laura thought again about the phone call she had received from Cynthia on Monday night. She had felt relieved that Cynthia had found and photographed the list and the other documents that gave details of the prospective blackmail victims' previous crimes. She had tried to dismiss the thought that in order to do so, Cynthia had broken into what was now Claire's house. This, she knew, was wrong... but did the end result justify the means? She really hoped it would.

This evening Cynthia had also told her about the break-in at her house on the previous night and the threatening messages that she had found. Cynthia had said she strongly suspected Claire and her man friend were the blackmailers, and that she would have the photos giving proof of Claire's involvement by the weekend. What was really important was that she now needed to find out the identity of Claire's man friend. She only hoped Mr Collinson could help.

Laura felt guilty as she reflected on this information. To think that Julia's baby sister could stoop so low and that all of this would never have happened if she...' 'Stop it!' she said loudly. 'You cannot change what is. Help if you are needed, otherwise let Cynthia deal with it.'

Think of something else, she told herself. So she thought about Mr Collinson and his job, such a pleasant friendly man. But to discover that they might have an arsonist in the village? Who could it be? With a frown, Laura tried to think of a senior lady who would fit the pattern of events. It was no use, she was too tired. Her mind flitted from the dinner at Cynthia's, to the Christmas party and Mrs Mould's outrageous performance at the church hall, and she shuddered. She really must try and find a way of keeping Mrs Mould from alcohol in future.

As for Mr Mould? He had been very rude when he'd collected his wife from the church hall. True, she had confronted him and told him to look at his own faults before criticizing his wife. He had glared at her for a second and then his glance had slid away.

'Don't keep thinking of Mr Mould again,' Laura muttered. 'You know he is bad for your blood pressure.' So she thought about the new vicar, the Reverend George Wilson, and clicked her tongue. He was so unlike her friend Arthur. He had stormed out of the Church Hall today leaving her to cope with an inebriated Mrs Mould, a furious Mr Mould and three broken tables. Her lips tightened, she would have words with him tomorrow. It was all very well giving everyone orders from on high, but she really did feel it was about time he stopped being so self-righteous and did some of the hands on work himself.

Something niggled at the back of Laura's mind as though she had forgotten something. What was it? She frowned and rubbed her temples with her fingertips, her eyes felt itchy and she realized that she was not thinking rationally. She needed some sleep. She got to her feet, went into the kitchen and made her nightly cocoa. As for what Mr Collinson had told her about an arsonist? She sighed. There was some tiny detail she was forgetting. If only she could remember. Well, she thought, as she sipped her bedtime drink, tomorrow is another day. She would deal with that problem then.

Chapter Thirty Three

Saturday evening

Alfredo did a last minute check of the glassware and the table covers in his restaurant and as he did so, his thoughts went back to the information that Cynthia Roberts had given him this morning and his face darkened with anger. He thought about the blackmail payment he was due to make a week on Sunday. At least now it might not happen.

Cynthia had told him that she recognised the woman who was one of the blackmailers and that she was trying to find out who the woman's male partner was. Well if that was so, it was time to do something about it. He was not going to pay the money, it was time this evil came to an end. A plan began to form in his mind as he flicked through the reservations book. He would think it through and deal with it later. In the meantime, he checked his watch – 6.40pm and so far no cancellations for tonight. He nodded in satisfaction; they had twelve sets of reservations throughout the evening which meant it would be quite busy. He stood for a while thinking about the blackmailers, and watching John, the waiter, checking the silverware. Then, without warning, his thoughts returned to Wednesday night when he'd met up with Martha.

Such a pretty, feminine lady and the Golden Rose Tea Shoppe was thriving. But it was not only the mutual attraction and business interest that had drawn them together, it was the discovery that they were both being blackmailed. Somehow, the very fear of this threat had made them closer than ever.

Martha had told him briefly of the reason for her blackmail and he, in turn, had told her about the Sheffield scandal. Neither of them had probed too deeply, but strangely their mutual problems had comforted them. Alfredo smiled as he thought about that. They had agreed on Wednesday night that they would tackle the problem together.

He glanced up at the restaurant clock – it was coming up to seven and the first early bird customers were due to arrive any minute.

The phone rang and he picked up the receiver. 'Lorenzo's Restaurant,' he announced.

'Alfredo, is that you?' asked a weepy voice which he instantly recognised. 'Yes, Martha. What is it?' He could hear her sobbing.

'You just won't believe what's happened.' The sobs became louder.

'What? When? Where?' He asked in alarm.

'I just... well, I can't explain. Can you come along here?'

'Of course,' he slammed down the receiver, called out to John, 'I'll be back in a few minutes,' then pulled on his coat and rushed out of the door and down the High Street.

Martha was standing trembling outside her café as he raced towards her. As he approached she pointed numbly at the cafés plate glass window. There in letters a foot high and in bold white paint was the message:

The owner of this café is a lying bitch

Alfredo stared at it then hugged Martha to him as she sobbed into his shoulder.

'So now the whole village will know.'

'When did this happen?' he asked, 'surely if the café was open someone would have noticed?'

Martha answered in a muffled voice, 'I closed at 5.30. There was nothing then, it was already dark and I wouldn't have noticed now except that I went to put the empty milk bottles out a few minutes ago.' She wiped away her tears and looked up at him, 'what will people think?'

Cautiously, Alfredo touched the writing on the window. It was still wet. 'They won't think anything,' he said, 'not if you and I act quickly. This is whitewash, not real paint. So let's fetch some buckets of water and get to work.'

They scrubbed furiously at the window until all traces of the message had disappeared. Alfredo stood back and eyed the glass critically. 'So, that's all clean now.' He smiled at Martha and gave her another reassuring hug. 'You see. We have dealt with it!'

Martha still looked frightened. 'But what if he or she returns?'

'Not tonight, they won't.'

She looked up at Alfredo. 'I'm sure this is the blackmailers work. But what about you? If someone has done this to me, there's no telling what they've got planned next? Plus, haven't you got to leave the money up at the cemetery next Sunday?'

Alfredo's expression became stern. 'It is not going to happen. I will phone Cynthia Roberts on Monday and let her know.'

Martha said worriedly, 'You mean you're going to ignore the threats?'

Alfredo looked at her then smiled coldly, 'I have a plan,' he said.

He took off his overcoat, put it round her shoulders and took her arm, 'Now lock up your café, you're coming with me.'

'But I've not cashed up.'

'Let's do that then,' Alfredo said. They went back into the café and when Martha had dealt with the takings, she locked up and they made their way back to the restaurant.

'You need some good warm food inside you,' Alfredo said as they walked along. 'Didn't you know that eating food often helps to soothe the nerves?'

Thirty minutes later Martha pushed back her plate and said, 'That was wonderful Alfredo, I'm so full I probably won't eat again until Monday.'

'But you'll take another glass of wine?' he asked. 'It will help relax you after so much stress.' He poured more wine and stroked her hand gently, 'better now?'

'Yes, thanks to you.' She smiled at him then said, 'I suppose this means I've got to make you lots more butterfly buns.'

He grinned, 'Of course and lots more of your bilberry tarts please.'

They both burst out laughing and clutched each other's hands. For a second Alfredo gazed at Martha, then he leaned forward and gently pressed his lips to her wrists.

Martha cleared her throat but did not pull away. 'Now what's all this about you not going to that meeting at the cemetery next Sunday?'

Alfredo leaned even closer and whispered, 'My plan will include you and some others. But first I will talk to Cynthia Roberts and I must think it out carefully.'

'Just what are you going to do?'

He kissed her fingertips and smiled, 'When I have worked it all out in detail, you'll be the first to know.'

Chapter Thirty Four

Neill waved to Miss Windle, gave a short beep on the car horn, then drove back to Cynthia's house. As he would be working in Sheffield on Monday he needed to get the details from Cynthia about Claire Forbes and her supposed boyfriend. Hopefully, once he'd located Claire's old digs, he might manage a chat with her landlord and perhaps glean some more information about her boyfriend.

He parked the car and looked out at the lighted windows of Cynthia's house. It had been so good meeting up with her again. As well as Cynthia being very attractive, she was a bright, hard-working woman and he was impressed by the fact that she'd had the courage to set up in business on her own. He'd been stunned when Cynthia had told him about Harry's death. On the few occasions that he'd met Harry, he'd grown to like his straight forward manner. Harry had been a hard-headed business man and whilst he could be blunt at times, there was no doubt that he'd thought the world of Cynthia.

Neill looked out at the lighted windows again and felt a sense of pleasure and gratitude that fate had brought him back to her once more. She had always been his friend and in the past, when she was training to do P.I. work, she had often asked him for advice on such matters.

But now both their lives had changed. It was over three years since his divorce and he'd had various short term relationships since then, but maybe, because of his job, and, some ladies had said, because of his inquiring mind, they had not lasted long. Not many women really understood what the working life of an insurance investigator was about, and how he could be called away to different parts of Britain at short notice. His occupation was hardly the kind to ensure a quiet domestic home life. Would Cynthia understand? Hope surged in his heart; his work would be unlikely to worry her since she was in a similar profession herself, but the important question was did she see him as a friend, or was there a possibility of something more? Doubt clouded his mind, so many questions without any answers. There was only one way to find out. He would need to be cautious, Cynthia had only been widowed for a year and he knew just how much she had loved Harry. Could love come along twice in their lives? 'I hope so,' he told himself, 'but don't go charging in there making her feel that just because you are helping her she has to be more than a friend to you.' He sighed, glanced in the car mirror and straightened his tie, then got out of the car and went back into Cynthia's house.

Cynthia turned to smile at him as he came into the kitchen. 'That didn't take too long, did it?' she said. 'Didn't Miss Windle invite you in and offer you a bedtime drink?' she asked as she handed him a tea-towel.

'No,' Neill said, 'I think she guessed I was in a bit of a hurry to get straight back.' He looked down at the tea-towel and grimaced, 'I should have taken more time, then I wouldn't have got roped into drying the dishes.'

'Well now,' Cynthia frowned in mock indignation, 'you didn't really expect a three course meal for free, did you?'

'That's the trouble with you women, always getting the last word,' Neill grinned.

She laughed as she cleared away the crockery. 'Not always, sometimes we win, sometimes we lose.' She walked past him and into the living room. 'Come and sit down a minute and let me get you a coffee before you go.' She looked at him enquiringly, 'or perhaps something stronger?'

He followed her and sat down. 'No, nothing at all thanks, don't want to get drowsy when I'm driving at this time of night.'

'Okay then.' Cynthia went to fetch her brief case, 'let's get down to business.' She brought out a sheet of paper from the brief case and joined him on the sofa. 'This is the Sheffield address of Claire Forbes' former digs and I've also made a note of what I overheard whilst I was... umm,' she cleared her throat. 'How shall I put it? Er, 'visiting' Claire's house?'

'Naughty girl,' Neill grinned but warned, 'in future be very careful with that kind of caper, because if you should get caught...'

'I know, I know,' Cynthia interrupted. 'But I didn't, and now I'm sure from what was said that this boyfriend of Claire's has some connection with retailing. There was a mention of selling Christmas trees and about it being opposite the florist's shop. And you heard Miss Windle mention what she had seen, and she never misses anything. As for Claire's bedroom, I've jotted everything down as I heard it. I just hope you can make sense of it. I took the photos that I'd taken of the list and the other papers to the chemists. They'll be ready to pick up at the weekend.'

Neill glanced at the papers and stood up. 'Right, I'll go over this again before I leave on Monday. What we really need to find out is this man's name. Once we have that, we're in business.'

Cynthia looked up at him. 'Going already?' It was so great to have Neill helping her on these cases, she just hoped he didn't think she was using him because of their former friendship.

'Needs must,' Neill replied. 'I've got some other stuff to sort out before I leave on Monday, but I'll phone you on Monday evening and let you know what progress I've made.' He made his way into the hall.

Cynthia followed him and lifted his overcoat from the hall stand. 'Better put this back on, it's getting cold out there tonight.' She felt a warm glow of affection as she watched him reach for his coat and put it on. On an impulse she stretched up, gave him a hug and kissed him lightly on the cheek. 'Thank you so much for...' but before she could finish her sentence he'd pulled her into his arms and kissed her firmly on the mouth. Then, just as quickly, he pushed her away and opened the door. She felt her heart pound and speechless, she stared up at him. 'What was…?'

'Goodnight Cynth,' he said breathlessly. 'I'll phone you Monday evening; hopefully I'll have more information by then.' He turned and strode out of the door.

Cynthia stood in the doorway and watched as he drove off without even a wave goodbye. She closed the door quietly and leaned against it for a while. She felt strangely breathless. Why had he been so abrupt? She knew from past experience that that had been much more than a friendly kiss, but, more worryingly, why was her pulse racing like this?

*

Neill pressed hard on the accelerator and gripped the steering wheel angrily. 'You idiot!' he growled, 'why did you do something as stupid as that? Now you've probably frightened her off.' He stared angrily at the road ahead as he drove along. What was he going to do? Should he phone her when he got home and apologize? Or should he just do nothing and wait to see how she reacted when he phoned on Monday night. The last thing he wanted was to upset her. 'Just wait and see what happens,' he muttered. 'Yes, I know I'm taking the coward's way out, but it certainly will be the safest.'

Chapter Thirty Five

Sunday morning

Laura awoke with a start. Was that the telephone ringing? Who on earth would be phoning her at 7am on a Sunday morning? She squinted at the alarm clock, then in disbelieve sat bolt upright, put on her spectacles and stared at the clock again. 9.15! Good heavens! For the first time in years she had overslept. Not only that, she had forgotten to set the alarm.

The phone continued to ring relentlessly so she pulled on her dressing gown and hurried downstairs to answer its call, only to find that it stopped the moment she reached it. She stared down at it in annoyance. That call was sure to be from the vicar demanding to know who was going to pay for the ruined tables in the church hall. Well, he would just have to wait. She had already missed the Sunday morning service and she was in no mood to discuss church expenses right now.

Twenty minutes later she sat at the breakfast table and having finished her porridge, began to open yesterday's mail. Saturday had been so busy that she have simply tossed the post on the table, but there hadn't seemed to be any letters that looked important. She discovered that five of them were indeed letters from different charities appealing for more contributions. There was also a letter from a funeral firm offering to pre-plan her funeral, so there was little to put her into a joyous mood. The charity letters she put to one side, she would reply to them later. She pondered over the funeral letter for a while and wondered whimsically what would happen if she, on taking up this offer, was to leave this mortal coil before she had completed the easy payments. Would they then only deliver half a funeral? Perhaps with no handles on the casket or only half a wreath? She smiled and tossed the letter into the waste paper basket.

As she cleared away the breakfast things her thoughts returned to the previous day. It had certainly been one of the most eventful days of the year. The disaster at the church hall all but guaranteed that she wouldn't forget that Christmas party in a hurry. Better not to think about that anymore. Her thoughts moved on to the lovely dinner at Cynthia Robert's house and to the meeting of Mr Collinson – such a charming and intriguing man. She felt flattered that he had asked for her help in his enquiries, she would certainly try her hardest, but where should she begin?

Going into the living room she went to her desk, unlocked it and got out the books that gave details of the members of all the community groups in the area. Somewhere in these books there would be information about new members that had joined the groups over the last few years. What she was looking for was someone amongst these newcomers who might well match the profile of the suspected arsonist.

For a minute she thought about the new blind piano-tuner that she had seen a few weeks ago – she had certainly been suspicious of him. There was something about him that was not quite right. In fact, judging by what she had noticed then, she did not think that he was blind at all. Laura frowned. Now she thought about it, since his arrival she had heard rumours around the village that small, but valuable ornaments had disappeared shortly after his piano-tuning visits. However, as far as she knew, he had not been seen in the area during these last two weeks and she could not accuse him of being an arsonist suspect seeing as he most definitely was not a female pensioner.

Sitting down, she picked up the first book. 'Hmm,' she read out loud, 'The Gardening club, let us see what we can unearth from here.'

Two hours later Laura, with a sense of finality, put down the last book which gave membership details of the Bonfire and Firework Club, and felt a sense of despair. There had not been a glimmer of a suspect amongst them. She had had high hopes about finding someone in this group, reasoning that any arsonist would be attracted to this kind of entertainment. But no, all of the members were male, with the exception of one lady who turned out to be thirty years old and who had only joined because she loved fireworks.

What to do now? Laura rested her head on her hands and stared down at the discarded stack of books. She had been through them all, from the Gardening Club right through to the Mother's Union and the Flower Arranging Group, convinced that any newcomer to the village would be only too glad to join one group or another in an effort to make new friends. But this did not seem to be the case. 'So think again,' she told herself. 'If a person did not join groups then this usually means that the character is an introvert.' And that could make life difficult. How then could she find a suspect arsonist? Surely the woman must be interested in something, even if it was only watching the TV.

Laura thought about this. The BBC often ran shows on painting and drawing, and lately they even did cookery classes. She clearly remembered watching a cookery programme the other week where the chef demonstrated a new recipe for steak and kidney pudding which was very interesting...

Wait! Where had she heard someone remark on steak and kidney puddings before? It must have been recent. There was something else. And it had been annoying. What was it? Where was it? And when?

There had been some part of the conversation or the situation that had irritated her, but relating to what? 'Think about something else,' she said, 'then it will come to you.' Laura thought about the beginning of the week, about her interview with the school Headmistress and little Penny-Ann, and about the tall thin blackmailer, but they had not discussed food. Yet she was sure someone somewhere had said 'steak and kidney pudding for tea tonight.' No, that was not quite right. They had said, 'steak and kidney pudding for *his* tea tonight.' Of course!

It had been Mrs Edna Thackeray, the lodger who lived with Mr Mitchell, the florist. Why had they been discussing food? Because on her way home she had seen Edna Thackeray building yet another bonfire in the back garden, and Edna had said that she was making steak and kidney pudding for Mr Mitchell that night. Laura thought about this woman and frowned. Of course! The bonfire had been the cause of her irritation, not the pudding. The woman was forever building bonfires in Mr Mitchell's garden. In fact, she drove her neighbours mad because she kept making fires whenever they hung their washing out. She should warn them at the very least.

Could such a bustling, hard-working little woman like Edna Thackeray be an arsonist? It seemed such a preposterous idea. But then, Laura reminded herself, these days burglars hardly went round wearing striped jumpers and eye masks either. She stared down at the books in front of her. Was this just a desperate guess because she could not find anyone else to would fit the pattern of an arsonist? 'You must be logical,' she said. 'You need facts before jumping to any serious conclusion.'

Thinking back, she remembered the day when she had first met Edna Thackeray. She had seen a nervous little woman gazing worriedly at the notice board outside the Post Office where vacant rooms and bed-sits were advertised. Now that had been in December 1969, just before...

'Stop! Don't start thinking of Julia again,' she muttered sternly to herself. 'Concentrate on Edna Thackeray.' Yes, the woman had told her she was staying at a Leeds hotel and that she was looking for something much quieter, perhaps a flat or a room here in Fawdon. And she had recommended Mr Mitchell's establishment. Laura remembered feeling that Mr Mitchell might well appreciate some female company, as well as a paying tenant, since his *friend* Adrian had left him recently in very suspicious circumstances.

She clasped her hands to her mouth. What had she done? Had she in fact encouraged a pyromaniac to come and live here in this village? Was Edna Thackeray an arsonist? The only facts she had was that the woman had moved here in 1970 and that she liked making bonfires, but that wasn't sufficient evidence.

She frowned, where should she start? Firstly, she would have to phone Cynthia and tell her of her suspicions, but then there would be much more that they would need to find out about Edna Thackeray.

Chapter Thirty Six

Monday evening
7pm.

Simon perched on a stool in his darkened shop and picking up his binoculars, focused on the premises across the road. The large white poster had been removed from the shop window and there was finally movement inside. He could see two men moving about and arranging their stock. What he could not see in detail, and this was most frustrating, were the prices of the items that were being displayed. The problem was that in order to do so he would have to move closer, much closer. He heard the sound of the flat door opening and a beam of light shot across the shop floor. 'Close the door,' he hissed, and looking round saw Edna coming towards him with a tray of tea and biscuits. 'What's all this?'

'I've brought you a warm drink in case you planned to stay here spying all night,' Edna said.

'Thank you very much, but I am not spying, I'm just... observing.'

'Well, observing or spying, your dinner's back there in the oven and it'll be dried as old boot before too long.' She reminded him.

Simon took a grateful sip from his tea. 'What you don't seem to understand, Edna, is that my 'spying' as you call it, is important. You see in business, you have to know what your competitors are up to.'

Edna stared at him. 'Why don't you just go look?' She nodded at the premises opposite, 'it's only a stone's throw away.'

'That wouldn't be right, would it? I mean, they might think I was being nosy.' He peered again through the binoculars. 'Besides, those blokes are much bigger than I am.'

'Would you like me to go?' Edna said. 'I could take a notebook and pen and write all the prices down for you.'

Simon looked horrified. 'They wouldn't like that. And besides, they know you live here so they'd probably send you packing.' His gaze strayed again to the lighted shop window across the road, then moved on to the large white van that was parked up alongside the premises. He knew for a fact that the van had not been unloaded and his suspicions deepened. Those blokes were up to something rotten, he could feel it in his gut.

'If you're going to stay in here all night I could bring you a flask and a blanket,' Edna's voice reached him.

'Course I'm not,' he finished the last of his tea and handed her the tray.

'It's just... we need a good excuse you see.' For a moment he stared down at the tray that Edna was holding, then he smiled up at her. He had it!

'Think Trojan Horse! No, that's not quite right. Think American hospitality. Over there when folk move in, what do the neighbours do?'

Edna thought for a while then said. 'From what I've seen in the films they take them casseroles, either that or an apple pie.' She looked at Simon worriedly, 'we've only got jam roly-poly.'

'But you make a mean cup of tea,' Simon said excitedly. 'So, what if you were to make up a nice brew and add a few chocolate digestives, then you could got over there and...'

'And what? Spy for you?' Edna said.

'I don't quite see it as spying,' Simon said huffily. 'In business it's called price comparison – all the big supermarkets do it.'

'But you're not a supermarket, you're a florist.' Edna replied.

Simon looked irritated. 'I am quite aware of that,' he said. 'But I also hear that they are going to sell plastic holly and wreaths, stuff that *I* would never touch. What worries me are the plants they have in the window. Are they real or artificial? I'd like to know what price they are and, more importantly, I want to know what the hell is in that big white van.' Snatching up the binoculars again he said, 'Look, there's a bloke going round to the van. Yes! The doors are opening...'

'If he's unloading you won't have long to wait then,' Edna said.

'Edna, I'm almost sure those blokes have got Christmas trees in there. What I need to know is what sizes the trees are, if they're cut or rooted, and most importantly, what price they are?'

'Will the trees have price tickets on them?'

'Not yet, but if you look around when you're over there, welcoming the proprietor to the neighbourhood as it were, you might just happen to notice if there's a few price cards or a price list lying around.'

'I'll go make a pot of tea and switch the oven off then,' Edna hesitated and looked at him uneasily. 'You sure you don't want to go? You know what to look for.'

'Ah, but they'd be suspicious of me. They'd never harm a little old lady.'

Edna shot a wary look at him before she headed towards the flat door.

He called after her. 'There'll be no need to worry, I'll be right here watching over you.' He heard a distinct snort as the flat door closed behind her.

Ten minutes later Simon watched as Edna, now dressed in a thick coat and scarf, trotted across the road bearing a tea tray. She knocked on the shop door and he saw a man come and open it. Then she went into the shop and disappeared from view. Simon checked his watch – it was 7.25pm exactly. He'd give her twenty minutes, half an hour at most… and then what? What would he do if she didn't return? He thought about this and decided that if she didn't come back after half an hour, he'd call the police and report a suspected burglary. After all, no way could he tackle two blokes by himself. 'Coward!' An inner voice niggled at him. 'I am not!' He retorted loudly, 'I'm just being logical.' Nevertheless, he stood with his eyes fixated on the shop door opposite, waiting for the sturdy figure of Edna to re-emerge. Every few seconds his gaze switched from there to the clock and with each passing minute, his anxiety increased.

7.35pm. She'd been gone ten minutes but it seemed like an hour. Simon chewed on his lip. She should be on her way back by now. And where were the two blokes? How long did it take them to drink a cup of tea?

The men were no longer visible in the shop window and they weren't out at the van, so where the hell had everyone got to? He opened the shop door, walked outside and stood shivering on the edge of the pavement. He felt cold and angry. He should have gone himself, rather than sending a helpless old woman. Suddenly he remembered what the Romans used to do to messengers, especially if they thought they were up to no good. He gasped in horror. What had he done? Enough was enough. Drawing himself up to his full height, he started to cross the street.

At that precise moment, the shop door across the road opened and Edna Thackeray, carrying a large package, came out. She hurried towards him and they made their way back home. Once inside the shop, Simon bolted the door and turned to her. 'What happened?' he asked anxiously. 'Are you ok? Did you get the prices?'

Edna eased the package onto the counter and said, 'One thing at a time Simon.' Taking a deep breath she added, 'Yes, I'm alright, and yes, I managed to spot some prices.' Then she said delightedly, 'But just look at what they gave me.' She unwrapped the package to reveal a large plastic poinsettia.

Simon stared at it in horror.

'Don't know why you're pulling a face like that,' Edna said. 'This doesn't need watering, it only needs dusting.'

'I can only insist that you keep that *thing* in your room, I will not tolerate it in my showroom.'

'Nobody asked you to,' Edna replied. 'They gave it to me. Now, I saw the list and I've memorised as many prices as I can, do you want to know them before I forget them?'

'Yes please.' Simon snatched up a pen and paper. 'Start with the Christmas trees.'

'There wasn't a price ticket on them, they seemed to be pricing them by the foot. I thought they were very reasonable.'

'Well they would be, wouldn't they,' Simon said irritably, 'especially if they've been nicked.'

'Are you going to let me finish? Edna asked, 'because my memory's not that reliable.'

'Go on then, the prices?'

'Three foot trees at 25p a foot, five foot trees 30p a foot and six foot trees at 35p a foot.' She looked at Simon, 'There seemed to be an awful lot of them. The van was choc-a-block with trees as well.'

'Blimey!' Simon gasped, 'that works out at 75p for a three foot tree. It's miles cheaper than I can buy them.'

'I'm only telling you what I saw,' Edna said indignantly. She looked again at her plastic poinsettia and smiled. 'Speaking for myself I thought this was very generous of them.' With that remark she picked up the plant, opened the flat door and left him with his thoughts.

Simon watched as the door closed behind her, then turned to look bleakly at the premises opposite. What on earth was he to do? His Christmas trees, which he'd already ordered and paid for, were due to be delivered by Barry, the grower, later in the week. What was he to tell his customers who, in all good faith, had placed their orders? He could hardly undercut the prices of the shop opposite without losing a lot of money himself. And, most importantly, how would his customers react when they saw his competitor's prices?

For a while he stared out at the shop opposite until its lights finally went out and then he realised there was little point in standing there. He walked back into his flat and thought about his supper, now stone cold in the oven. This had not been a good day. 'Sleep on it,' he told himself firmly, although he knew he'd probably have nightmares about Christmas trees.

Chapter Thirty Seven

Monday evening

Cynthia replaced the telephone receiver thoughtfully than sat for a while pondering the information that Miss Windle had just given her. Not that it was anything definite, but it was a lead. Neill would find out more. But at least as far as arsonists in Fawdon were concerned, this lady could be considered a suspect. She glanced up at Gertie, the grandmother clock – 8.25pm. Neill had said he would ring tonight, in fact she'd thought he would have rang much earlier.

Her mind went back to when she had last seen him on Saturday night and she thought about the kiss he had given her and once more, she felt her pulse begin to race. She knew from past experience that the kiss had hardly been just a friendly one, it had been something more.'

The phone rang, startling her and she snatched up the receiver.

'Hello Cynth,' said Neill.

Feeling breathless as she heard his voice, she answered, 'Hello Neill, I was wondering what…'

'Sorry I'm late phoning, I've only just got back into Leeds. The traffic was hell. The roads were packed and it was starting to snow in Sheffield.'

'It's still clear here,' Cynthia said. 'Least it was when I came home. Anyway how are you, and do you have any news?'

'Indeed I do, my lovely.' She heard him laugh, 'Seems like you've got a right pair of crooks there. Seriously though, they've both got records, but the man's is far worse than the woman's.' He paused, 'you need to be careful there, Cynth.'

'I will. Go on then. Have you got his name?'

'Yes, it's Lennie Stones. I got that from Claire Forbes's landlord. And did he have some stories to tell. He knew Lennie long before he joined up with Claire. Apparently Lennie's been locked up loads of times, mainly for burglary, but often for assault too. As for Claire, her landlord claimed she was no angel, that she'd been done for shoplifting and she was known to the Sheffield police for assault and drunken behaviour. I got the impression from her landlord that Claire had not been with Lennie all that long as he'd only been out of prison for five months. Anyway, once I had his name I checked with the estate agent who leased him those shop premises in Fawdon. Did you know it is only on a short term lease?'

'No, but I think I can guess why, he'll be gone by the time summer comes.'

'He'll be gone long before that if we can prove he's the blackmailer.'

'Good, because one of my clients is meeting the blackmailer next Sunday, at the cemetery of all places, so I'll talk to him and see what we can arrange.'

'That's great,' Neill replied. 'Remember, I'm always here if you need me.' There was a silence and then he said, 'have you any news for me?'

'A little, but nothing definite,' Cynthia replied, 'Miss Windle phoned me tonight with a very interesting theory…'

Chapter Thirty Eight

Tuesday morning
8.30 a.m

Simon Mitchell unlocked the shop door, went outside and stood for a moment, shivering. It was definitely getting colder, but still not a snowflake in sight. He sighed, it seemed ages since they'd had a white Christmas. His gaze drifted towards the shop across the road and he scowled. He'd been awake most of the night worrying about the whole Christmas tree situation, but he'd not found a solution. 'Think of something else,' he told himself, 'and get those nice chrysanthemums outside, they're sturdy enough to stand up to this kind of weather.' And he traipsed back into the shop to get the flowers.

Two hours later, he'd just finished making some holly wreaths when the shop doorbell tinkled and Simon looked up to see Cynthia Roberts standing at the counter. 'Well hello Mrs Roberts,' he said as he hurried round the counter to greet her. 'It's a long time since I've seen you.'

Cynthia smiled at him, 'You've missed me then?'

'Of course! I don't know if it's right but I did hear that you're back in Fawdon and that you've set up your own Private Investigations business.'

'All of which is true,' Cynthia said.

'I was so sorry to hear about your husband,' Simon said quietly.

'Thank you. You're so kind.' Cynthia paused then quickly moved on. 'I'm sorry I've not been in to buy some of your gorgeous flowers, but I've been busy moving in and getting organised. However,' she smiled at him, 'things are settling down now so you'll soon be seeing me a bit more often.'

'That is cheering news,' Simon said. 'I've some lovely Christmas stock coming in daily...'

'Ah!' She interrupted, 'today I've come to see you about some different matters. We can get to the flowers later.'

Simon suppressed a sigh, 'As you will. How can I be of help?'

'Well, the first thing is that I'm looking for a part-time gardener, someone to sort out my back garden. I know they can't do much at this time of year, but I will definitely need someone in the spring. I wondered if you knew of anyone?'

He got out his notebook, leafed through it and thought about the gardeners he knew. He usually stuck a card in the shop window for them when they wanted a bit more work. But now, with Christmas being so near? At the thought of Christmas his mind jumped to the tree problem again. He stared up blankly at Mrs Roberts. She was a private eye wasn't she? She could be the one person who could help him.

'Have I got a smut on my nose or something?' Cynthia laughed.

'So sorry Mrs Roberts, only it has just occurred to me that you may be able to help me.' He pointed with his biro at the shop over the road. 'It looks like I may have some hassle with the new tenants over there, and I wondered...?' He hesitated, then said anxiously, 'I'm prepared to pay a fee of course.'

'What is the problem?' Cynthia asked.

Simon looked about him uneasily before he continued. 'I don't like to be unwelcoming to new businesses coming into Fawdon, but these blokes,' he nodded in the direction of the shop opposite, 'well, I just think they're no good.' He leaned towards her and said confidingly, 'In fact they are about to undercut the prices of my Christmas trees. Now before you tell me that business is business and so forth, I know that it's impossible for them to sell trees at such a low price, I mean 75p for a three foot tree? That is ridiculous. No grower would sell to me at such a price. I reckon the truth is those trees have been nicked.'

'Can you prove this?' Cynthia said.

'I'm sure I can. Y'see at this time of year a lot of crooks do a night raid on the growers' fields, bit like sheep rustling y'see, only with trees it's easier, guaranteed sales Christmas week and then they're gone. Barry, the grower that supplies me with the trees has been complaining that some of them have been nicked over the weekend.' He nodded in the direction of the shop opposite. 'Those trees could be part of the stock that's been stolen from Barry.'

'Could you get your supplier here?'

'Sure I could. He'll be able to identify them – all growers have their own way of marking them, y'see. Then we could really sort them.'

'We'll need absolute proof, Mr Mitchell,' Cynthia warned. 'So as soon as your supplier gets here please let me know. I need to talk to him.' She took out her note book, scribbled both her phone numbers on a page, then tore the it out and gave it to him.

'I'll call him now,' Simon said. He turned away and was about to go to the phone when Cynthia stopped him. 'Before you do that Mr Mitchell there is something else I wanted to ask you.'

'Please do, anything at all.'

'I understand that you have a lady lodger staying with you, a Mrs Thackeray, if I am correct?'

'Edna? Yes, a nice lady, been with me for about two years now, she's been a godsend in fact.' He patted his stomach. 'Spoils me rotten she does.'

'Is she in at the moment?'

Simon looked at his watch. 'She'll have gone shopping at this time of day. She's sure to be in this afternoon though. Shall I tell her you want to see her?'

Cynthia hesitated. 'Before she came here did she stay at a Leeds hotel?'

'I think so, in fact I might still have her card somewhere in my workbench drawer.'

Cynthia nodded. 'You could tell her I'll come back this afternoon.'

Simon eyed her thoughtfully then, unable to control his curiosity, asked, 'Would it be anything important?'

Cynthia smiled and shook her head as she made for the shop door. 'I'm sure she'll tell you about it later, Mr Mitchell.'

He called after her. 'I'll try and find a gardener for you, but it's likely to be for after Christmas.'

She nodded and the shop door closed behind her.

Simon walked over to his workbench and began to root around in the drawer. Finally he found the card. He fished it out and read the address. Sure enough it was for a residential Leeds hotel. Why, he wondered, did that seem important to Mrs Roberts. He sighed and put it back in the drawer. He had enough to worry about without adding something else to the list.

He picked up the phone and dialled a number. 'Hello Barry, it's me, Simon Mitchell. You know you said last week that someone had been nicking your Christmas trees? Yes, well, I may be able to do something about that. Can you get down here? On Saturday afternoon? Yes, I think that's ok. I'll call you back if not. Cheers for now.' He replaced the receiver, then looked at his watch. He'd better give Mrs Roberts an hour to get home and then he'd ring her.

*

The same afternoon

Simon had just finished off his cup of hot soup when the shop door opened and Mrs Roberts came in. This time she was accompanied by a man. He was tall, well built, with thinning curly hair. He had an air of authority about him; and in Simon's mind this always meant trouble.

Simon eyed him warily then smiled at her, 'No problems about meeting the grower on Saturday, Mrs Roberts?'

'It's as we arranged,' Cynthia confirmed, 'but now we're here on a different matter. We'd like to see Mrs Thackeray.' She turned and looked at the man accompanying her. 'This is my friend, Mr Collinson.'

Simon nodded as the man shook his hand. 'Nice to meet you,' he murmured.

'About Mrs Thackeray?' Cynthia prompted, 'is she home yet?'

'Think so,' Simon said, 'I'll go and see.'

They watched him go through to the flat and heard the faint sound of knocking on a door and the murmur of voices.

A few minutes later Simon, accompanied by Edna Thackeray, came into the shop. Simon said, 'this is Mrs Roberts, Edna. She's a private investigator.'

Edna looked at her anxiously. 'You wanted to see me?'

'We just wanted to ask you a few questions Mrs Thackeray.' Cynthia said. She looked around. 'Is there somewhere more private perhaps, where we can talk?'

'Yes,' Edna replied. 'Best place is my room. If you'll come with me?'

She walked to the door which connected to the private quarters and ushered them through.

Simon said, 'Do you want me to come with them?'

Edna turned to look at him, then said resignedly, 'If you wish.'

Mr Collinson cleared his throat. 'This is rather a personal matter.'

'I want Mr Mitchell to be with me, he has the right to know,' Edna insisted.

'As you wish,' the man replied.

'I'll just bolt the shop door,' Simon called after them, 'shan't be a minute.' What on earth has Edna been up to? He wondered as he hurried after them to her room.

Edna looked around as Simon came in and she smiled weakly at him. 'Please sit down, all of you,' she said.

The man sat down and began. 'Mrs Thackeray, I'm Neill Collinson and I'm employed by the Detrice Insurance Company.' He handed her his business card.

Simon saw that at his words Edna's face had turned pale. She began to pluck at her apron nervously. 'What do you want from me?' she asked.

'I'll try to be brief,' the man said. 'The insurance company has received compelling new evidence about a claim you made three years ago on your house fire. As I understand it the house was burned to the ground?'

Edna nodded.

'Also,' Mr Collinson continued, 'I understand that your husband, a Mr Sidney Thackeray died in the fire?'

'Look, I thought this was all sorted,' Edna protested.

'So did we,' Mr Collinson sighed and he opened his briefcase and brought out some papers. 'That is until recently when the Detrice Company received a letter from a Mr William Smithson…'

'Him!' Edna blurted, 'Bill Smithson! They shouldn't take no notice of him. He was my husband's cousin, our only relative, and he's a wrong un, he is.'

'Nevertheless,' the man re-read the letter, 'he claims that the fire and Mr Sidney Thackeray's death were by no means accidental.'

'Go on, I'll bet he said I'd murdered him, didn't he?' Edna interrupted.

'You stated you thought your husband was dead,' Mr Collinson continued, 'and Mr Smithson claims that he was in prison at the time of the fire, but received a letter from Mr Thackeray, your husband, a few days later.'

'How could he? My Sidney was dead.'

Mr Collinson looked up at her. 'If you'll just let me finish telling you what he said.' He continued, 'Mr Smithson claims that your husband wrote to him stating that he was desperate for money and that he couldn't sell his house and he'd decided to get rid of it another way…' The man looked up at her again. 'Mr Smithson didn't receive this letter until a week after the fire.'

'My Sidney never wrote to Bill,' Edna protested, 'all Bill Smithson ever wanted from us was money. Always on the scrounge he is.'

'I understand your husband died in the house fire.'

Edna's lips trembled, 'He'd fallen. He'd been drinking y'see and he fell over trying to help me stop the blaze from getting any bigger. Anyhow he must have banged his head on the metal fender or something, 'cause he didn't get up. He just lay there. I shook him and shook him, but he wasn't breathing and the flames were near on top of us.' She gave a deep sigh. 'He was gone…'

'You left him there?' Mr Collinson asked.

Edna glared at him angrily, 'Do you think I'd leave anyone if I thought they were living? I was near burnt alive myself. As for Bill Smithson, since then he's haunted me. All he wants is money. He found out the insurance had paid up and he kept threatening me, saying I'm a killer and that he was going to tell everyone. And yes! I was scared see! So I gave him money, again and again and again.' She sniffed and wiped at her nose. 'I thought if he spoke up folk would believe him.'

'Why didn't you go to the police?' Mr Collinson asked.

'And knowingly rake all this stuff up again,' Edna shook her head, 'no, I just moved away.' She swallowed hard then said quietly, 'He found me again this year. Pretended to be a blind piano tuner, he did, though God only knows what other tricks he was up to. But this time I said no! And I'll tell you this, Mr insurance man, that Bill Smithson has spent more time in prison than out, you check his records, you'll see.'

Mr Collinson said, 'I understand what you're saying Mrs Thackeray, but we have this letter from him insisting that the fire was not accidental and that his cousin, Sidney Thackeray, was murdered. He claims to still have the letter that your husband wrote.' He sighed and got to his feet as Edna shook her head and began to sob.

Simon went to her and put his arms round her, trying to comfort her. 'Do you have to go on at her like this?' he protested angrily. 'Can't you see she's telling the truth?'

'I know you are trying to help Mrs Thackeray, Mr Mitchell.' Mr Collinson said, 'but I've my job to do. I will report my findings to the insurance company. I can't tell you what action they will take then, but I will notify Mrs Thackeray as soon as I have further news.' He looked at Mrs Thackeray with compassion then said gently, 'What you always have to remember is that according to our law, you are innocent until proven guilty.'

'And that won't take long, of course she's innocent' Simon growled. He hugged Edna to him. He watched while Mrs Roberts and the man got to their feet and said their goodbyes, then he guided them out through the shop and closed the door behind them.

'I'm sorry about all this.' Edna said as she followed him into the shop.

'Well, we know it's not true, that's for sure.'

Edna sobbed into her hankie, 'Yes,' she said, 'we know it's not true, but my problem is, how can I prove it?' She turned abruptly and ran off in the direction of her room.

'Don't worry Edna' he called after her, 'they'll get to the root of it, you'll see.' But all he heard in reply was the slamming of the door to her room. Simon stood silently for a while. So at last he'd found out why Edna had been frightened when she'd received a visit from the so-called blind man. With a bloody good reason as it turned out. That must have been Bill Smithson, and by making this claim what did that crook have to lose? Then another thought came into Simon's mind. More importantly, as Bill Smithson was the only surviving relative, what did he have to gain?

Chapter Thirty Nine

Wednesday afternoon

Laura sat on the bus on her way to Leeds and carefully placed the bunch of freesias on the seat beside her. Really, she thought, it would have been much better to have purchased the flowers at Kirkgate market in the city, but then she had wanted to call in on Simon Mitchell. She had tried her best to enquire tactfully about Mrs Thackeray in a carefully casual manner, but Mr Mitchell had seemed distracted and abrupt in his reply, so she had bought some flowers then made her way to the bus stop. Clearly, something was amiss.

She worried about this for a while and then she decided to visit Cynthia Roberts at her Leeds office when she had finished her Christmas shopping, and find out if her suspicions about Edna Thackeray were correct.

Leaning back in her seat she watched as the bus weaved its way through the heavy traffic towards the city centre. In a few minutes they would be approaching the Headrow where the large stores of Lewis's and Schofield's were situated. She would alight there and look for a nice present for her dear friend, Arthur. Laura smiled as she thought about him. He had been kind enough to invite her to stay with him in York over the Christmas period, and she was looking forward to it. She frowned, although she did hope that her visit would not make too much work for his housekeeper.

An hour later Laura eased herself into a seat in the Cosy Corner café and looked about her; this was her own little pre-Christmas treat. It would have been sensible of course to have ordered a light lunch, instead she sipped at the freshly ground coffee, eyed the fancy cake that the waitress had placed in front of her and smiled in satisfaction; she felt that this was well earned.

Glancing at her watch she noted the time, 1.30pm. She had checked the business address of Cynthia's premises in the phone book last week and, if she remembered correctly, her office was on the second floor. Fifteen minutes later Laura brushed the cake crumbs from her coat and got to her feet. She must be on her way.

*

The buzzer on the office door sounded sharply and Cynthia put down her pen, then got up and went to answer it. She felt puzzled, the postman had been this morning, and she had no further appointments for today. As she opened the door the smiling face of Miss Windle greeted her.

'Ah Cynthia' she said. 'I did wonder if I had pressed the correct button but that was silly of me. It clearly states on the door…'

'Miss Windle,' Cynthia said. 'Please, come on in.' She stood aside and allowed Miss Windle to precede her into the office. She watched her as she walked towards the desk, her sharp eyes taking in every detail of the room. Cynthia smiled; she knew very well that this lady would miss nothing. She said, 'Please sit down, Miss Windle, and I'll make us some coffee,' she hesitated, 'or would you rather have tea?'

'Tea if it's possible, Cynthia dear. I did have some excellent coffee earlier but I find that one cup of coffee a day is sufficient, and tea is so much easier to digest.' She turned to Cynthia and gave her the flowers, 'I thought this little gift might be appropriate for your place of work.' She looked at the Freesias, 'they are not ostentatious, yet they have such a refreshing perfume.'

As she took the flowers, Cynthia repressed a grin. I wonder where she bought these. I'll bet she's already visited Mr Mitchell's shop this morning. Then she said, 'How lovely, and how kind of you to think of me.' She looked around, 'I'm afraid I haven't got a vase here. Would you be offended if I put them in a milk bottle for the time being?'

'Not at all, my dear, but you shall have a vase by the weekend, I have dozens of them.'

Cynthia made the tea and then handed a cup to Miss Windle.

Taking a sip, Miss Windle sat back and looked at her. 'I am sure you must be wondering why I called in to see you.'

I think I can guess, Cynthia thought as she returned to her desk. Then she said, 'Not at all, it's nice to have visitors, and a good excuse to take a break from work.'

Miss Windle leaned forward and enquired. 'The truth is I did wonder if you had further news about the possible arsonist lady... Mrs Thackeray. You see I feel I may in some way be responsible for this... um, situation. Some years ago I did, in fact recommend Mr Mitchell's lodgings to her.'

Cynthia rearranged the flowers in the bottle. 'Did Mr Mitchell say anything?'

'Ah well,' Miss Windle cleared her throat, 'to be truthful Simon Mitchell was very busy this morning. In fact he seemed quite distracted, and I am not one to pry.' She looked across at Cynthia hopefully.

'Mr Mitchell may well have problems of his own,' Cynthia said. 'He is certainly not happy about the new tenants across the road.'

'Really? Is there any way that I could be of help?'

Cynthia pondered for a while. 'Yes, I'm going to ask you for a very small favour. It would certainly be of help to Mr Mitchell if you could do it. Can you come to his shop on Saturday afternoon, about 5.30pm?'

'Of course I will; would there be any connection with this favour and Mrs Thackeray?'

'I'm sorry, all I can tell you, about Edna Thackeray, Miss Windle, is that my colleague, Mr Collinson has the matter in hand.'

'Then Mrs Thackeray is being...?'

'As soon as I have Mr Collinson's permission to discuss this case, I will do so.' Cynthia saw the disappointment in Miss Windle's face and said, 'And I feel sure Mr Collinson appreciates the effort that you made on his behalf and that he'll want to thank you. Now,' she said, briskly changing the subject. 'I have some further news for you. I've been talking to Mr Lorenzo and I can tell you that you are about to receive an invitation from him for dinner on Sunday evening.' Cynthia paused and said meaningfully, 'I really hope you can come?'

Miss Windle's face lit up in surprise. 'I would be delighted to my dear, what time?'

'It'll all be on the invitation card and of course the food will be Italian.'

'Is it a special event? A birthday or something?'

'He was rather vague about that.' Cynthia's smile deepened into a grin. 'But I am sure it will be something special.'

Chapter Forty

Thursday Morning
11am

Peter Greystone was about half way through his mid-morning chocolate éclair when the shop bell buzzed. He spluttered a silent curse, wiped his mouth, made his way from his little back room into the shop, then stared in amazement to see his wife, Helen, standing at the counter.

Oh no, I'll bet she's found another house that she thinks I'll like, he thought. He said 'Now, what's up?' Another thought occurred to him. 'It's not the girls, is it?'

She shook her head and waved a cream coloured envelope at him.

At the sight of this his heart missed a beat – surely it wasn't that bloody blackmailer about to have another go at him. Then he noticed the colour of the envelope, it was not white as the other envelope had been, so he relaxed a little.

'Don't you want to know what's in it? Helen asked.

'I should think you're going to tell me,' Peter muttered, 'otherwise you'd not be standing there.'

'Don't be so grumpy,' she laughed, 'just because I spoiled your coffee break. What was it today, éclairs or apple slices?'

'Just tell me what's in the envelope, Helen.'

'It's an invitation to a dinner.'

'Aw no! Not another invite from some wholesaler trying to get rid of his pre-Christmas stock.'

'Will you let me finish?' Helen interrupted, 'it's nothing like that at all. It's from Lorenzo's Restaurant and you know how we like Italian food. Here, see for yourself.' She thrust the envelope at him and watched as he opened it and read the contents.

Peter smiled as he read the invitation. 'Well that is nice of Alfredo. He's says it's a special celebration. Does he mean it's his birthday?'

Helen shook her head. 'He's probably not mentioned that because he doesn't want us to feel obliged to buy him a present.'

'Still,' Peter said as he returned the invitation card to its envelope, 'Sunday evening is a bit short notice.' He looked at his wife. 'Are we going?'

'Of course we're going!' Helen said indignantly. 'Just how often do we get an invitation for a free dinner?'

The saying "there's no such thing as a free lunch" shot through Peter's mind, but he brushed it aside quickly. 'That's fine then, we'll go. But I don't see why you came all this way to tell me about it, you could just as easily have phoned me.'

Helen gazed at him, leaned on the counter and said softly. 'Well, the thing is, my darling, I'm a bit short on the housekeeping money this week, what with Christmas shopping and all, and if we're going to that dinner, I will definitely need a nice pair of shoes.' She smiled seductively at him and held out her hand.

'I should have known,' Peter grumbled. 'With you there always is a reason.' Then with an exaggerated sigh of reluctance he turned to reach for the petty cash box.

*

Thursday afternoon

Martha McPherson sat at her desk and fingered the cream coloured envelope thoughtfully, she'd already read the invitation and Alfredo had told her of his plans for Sunday evening. She felt a warm glow of affection as she thought about that; his confiding in her had been so reassuring. She thought about last Saturday night, he had been so wonderful helping her. She didn't know what she would have done if he had not come to the rescue. She realised that she was falling in love with Alfredo, and she was sure that he felt the same way about her... or did he?

On that evening he had been so helpful and so loving, and after a glass of wine or two, there had been no doubt in her mind how he felt. But this afternoon, on a bright winter's day, she was not quite so certain. She placed her elbow on the desk, rested her chin on it, and pondered. She had often heard the rumours about Italians being such Romeos, and. everyone knew that they were incredibly romantic and rarely faithful. But, she assured herself, Alfredo was not Italian. He was a

Yorkshire lad, born in Sheffield and brought up in Italy. There had to be a difference.

Feeling slightly better, Martha's thoughts moved on. Through the open office door she could hear the distant chatter of the customers and the clatter of the crockery as the waitresses cleared away. Business was brisk today, probably because of the good weather. At least now that she and Alfredo had come to a mutual agreement regarding their respective businesses everything was fine in the world. Or was it? Without warning, an unwelcome thought crept into her mind. She tried to dismiss it, but still it remained. It was a cynical thought and a nasty one, but what if deep down Alfredo was really only interested in her business and not her?

She jumped up angrily and strode into the café, 'Don't be so stupid!' she muttered. She stood silently for a while touching the scar on her neck then she forced a smile and nodded politely as she recognised some of her regular customers. You are really becoming paranoid, she told herself. Just because your first husband was cruel and a bully it doesn't mean that Alfredo is. Besides, you're not so perfect yourself.

Her mind went back to the fake notice she'd written almost two weeks ago and the earlier incident with the mouse droppings. Not that Alfredo's establishment had mice, but at the time she'd been so furious with him, and it had been so simple to pinch some droppings from her next door neighbour's pet mouse and slip them through Alfredo's letter box. She felt her face flush with guilt as she thought about that. She would have to confess to him. It was time that she did.

The smell of toasted teacakes reached her nostrils and she remembered that she'd not had any lunch. She looked down at her stocky body resignedly. Lunch was something she could afford to miss, she didn't want to get any bigger and it would be well worth the sacrifice. On Sunday she would be with Alfredo again, helping him, and, if things turned out right, most of her troubles would be over.

*

Thursday

Laura Windle opened her wardrobe door and peered inside it worriedly. It had been such a long time since anyone had invited her to a dinner. She had received invitations to Church Christmas and Easter functions galore, community suppers, of course. To say nothing of the annual Harvest festival event. But as for a recent formal invitation to a dinner?

Her expression softened into a gentle smile as she recalled the farewell dinner she had shared two years ago with her friend Arthur before he left for his new post in York. It had been a candlelit meal for two at a large hotel in Ilkley. To this day she could not remember what they had eaten, only that it had been good. All she could recall about that evening was the tenderness of Arthur and the bitter sweet feeling of knowing they were soon to part. Tears welled up in her eyes; she brushed them aside and bit down on her lip firmly. Don't keep looking into the past, she told herself, life moves on. Besides she would be visiting Arthur again soon. *'Life could have been so much better for you if you had just told Arthur the truth'* a voice in her mind reminded her. Laura shook her head. 'No' she said loudly, 'Arthur could not have accepted the fact that I am a blackmailer. He is too good a man for that.'

'He is also human,' argued the voice softly, *'and what is that saying about forgiveness being divine?'*

'I cannot undo the past,' Laura protested as she took several dresses out of the wardrobe and placed them on her bed. 'Now I am going to concentrate on the task in hand. Just what will be most suitable for Sunday evening? Now black is always correct for formal occasions.' She picked up the dress in question and held it up against herself in the mirror and her mouth tightened in distaste. 'No,' she said. 'It makes you look like an old crow. Perhaps the maroon coloured one might be better.' After some hesitation about the fit of the maroon dress, having recalled that on the last occasion she had worn it, it had felt rather snug, she finally decided upon a pale blue dress that would go well with her good pearls.

Having organised her wardrobe for Sunday evening, Laura's thoughts returned to Mrs Thackeray. She still felt anxious about having singled the woman out as a possible pyromaniac, but, she thought defiantly, she had been asked to do a job and she had done it to the best of her ability. Was there, she wondered, any connection between the forthcoming meetings at Mr Mitchell's shop on Saturday? And what would be the favour that Mrs Roberts expected her to do? She thought about Simon Mitchell, he had been so well behaved lately, ever since his dreadful *friend* Adrian had left him. She had always been of the opinion that having a lady lodger might in the end be much more suitable for a man with his... tendencies. But now how would the poor man feel if in fact Mrs Thackeray turned out to be an arsonist? Laura sighed in exasperation; she just wished she knew a little more about what was happening in Mr Mitchell's emporium. She felt sure that she could be of some help.

Chapter Forty One

Thursday evening
6pm

Simon Mitchell picked up the last remaining buckets of mixed bunches, hurried inside, and bolted the shop door behind him. What had started out as a bright and sunny day had dissolved into rain as evening came. It was cold and wet out there and he felt chilled to the bone. He only hoped that the rain wouldn't turn into black ice overnight. That would be all that he needed the week before Christmas. He put the buckets of flowers at the back of the shop and, with a weary sigh, went over to the till to cash up. He smiled as he counted the contents, as the takings were excellent. It had been a long and very busy day and he'd not eaten since 6am this morning, but at least he was seeing some reward for his hard work.

Having emptied the till, he switched off the interior lights and made his way back to his flat. He felt tired and hungry and wondered for a moment whether he should nip up to the chip shop on Horsefield Road to get some supper, but then he decided not to bother. Surely there must be something left in the fridge?

Five minutes later as he sat down to a cheese sandwich and a hot cup of tea, he thought about

Edna. He hadn't seen her all day and come to think of it, the last time she'd talked to him (and that had been through the closed door of her room) was on Wednesday morning. Then she'd said she was okay, and that she would see him later.

He'd knocked on her door this morning in the hope of asking her to stand in for him at lunchtime so that he could snatch a bite to eat, but there had been no answer and he had assumed that she'd gone out shopping. Now doubts formed a queue in his mind and he began to feel uneasy. What if after all this stress the woman was not well? What if she'd done something stupid? What if she was lying there, had been lying there all day and he'd not given a damn about her? Enough was enough, he'd best find out. Simon got to his feet and hurried along the corridor to her room. Knocking on her door, he called softly 'Edna? Edna? Come on love, open up... Are you alright?' There was no answer. He knocked louder, then pounded with the flat of his hand on the door. 'Come on Edna' he shouted. 'Open the door!' He waited; there was only silence. Fear grew in Simon's mind and he turned and raced back to his living room and to his desk where he kept all the keys. Picking out the right one he hurried back again to Edna's room. He knocked once more, just to be sure... no answer. He inserted the key in the door and went in.

As he switched on the light he looked around. The room had been stripped of Edna's belongings. There was no sign of her knitting magazines or the sweetie jar that she kept on the coffee table. The old family photographs which had graced the walls had vanished, even the fruit bowl was empty. Quickly he checked the wardrobe and the en-suite bathroom, but all traces of Edna had gone. Not a scarf or a hankie to be seen; he could not even find a toothbrush. As he went back into the room he noticed that the bed in the far corner was neatly stacked with clean sheets, blankets and towels and on top of them lay a note.

'What has she done?' he thought as he rushed towards the bed and picked up the note. It read:

Dear Simon,

I know you would do your very best to help me with this enquiry, but believe me the time has come when I have to deal with this myself. I know that I am not guilty of killing my Sidney and I didn't set our house alight on purpose. It was all a horrible accident. But as I told you on Tuesday afternoon, it is up to me to prove it. I'm going now because I don't want you to feel ashamed or embarrassed by my being here, living under your roof. I have written to Mr Collinson and told him where I will be staying so I'm not running away you see. I will get in touch with you when all of this is finally settled, so please don't worry. Thank you again for being a good landlord and such a very good friend.
Edna.

Simon tossed the note back on the bed and gave a loud sigh of exasperation. Why had she run away like this when he was doing his damnedest to help her? Of course she didn't kill her husband. No one could possibly believe that. As for her being a pyromaniac? Well the whole bloody idea of that was downright ridiculous. Though he had to admit there were times when he'd worried about the size of the bonfires she'd kept making in the back garden. She'd seemed to have some kind of fixation about them, but surely that was harmless. He hesitated and thought about that again; she definitely liked to see the flames, and she'd written in the note that *"she didn't set her house on fire on purpose."* What if it had happened here? He would have lost every. No! He dismissed the thought instantly. Edna was a good woman.

He gazed around the room again; there was nothing of her left, not even that bloody plastic poinsettia. She had been such a good lodger and such a good cook as well. She must have packed up and left through the back door. He felt a great sense of loss. He would miss her. Simon walked back into the corridor then, closing the door, locked it. He looked down at the key sadly; it had felt so final when he had done that. Slowly he went back into the kitchen. Now what was he to do? Advertise for yet another lodger? Not for a while he wouldn't. He had other things to deal with. He thought about the new traders across the road and his lips tightened. He would deal with them on Saturday.

Chapter Forty Two

Friday morning

Claire pulled her dressing gown about her and went to the door as she saw the postman coming up the drive. Hearing the flap of the letter box she wondered if there were any responses to her recent job applications. Bending down she picked up the envelope, opened it then stood silently reading the card.

'Anything for me?' Asked Lennie as he came into the hall and pulled on his coat.

Smiling broadly Claire turned to him. 'Guess what? It's a dinner invitation!'

'For me? Who from?'

'It's for me really,' Claire giggled, 'but as it says "and guest" I suppose you can come as well.' She walked up to him and pulled his coat collar up, tugging him towards her. 'If you're a good boy, that is.'

'Give us it here.' He snatched it out of her hand and read it. 'It's from that Italian restaurant in the High Street. Fancy him inviting us.'

'Isn't he one of our... clients?'

'He's one that's not coughed up yet, he should pay up this Sunday.'

'Maybe that's why he's inviting us. Still, if it's a free meal? And I would like to go.' Claire peered into the hall mirror and fluffed at her blonde hair.

'But I'll need to find a hairdresser fast, I'd best get one in town, can't go looking like this.'

'We'll go alright, but if he thinks he's getting away from paying by giving us a free meal, he's got another think coming,' Lennie said. He eased her to one side, admired his reflection and smoothed his sleek dark hair. 'After all, we know what we know, don't we girl. Thanks to your big sister.'

Claire frowned and looked at him anxiously, 'But our little side-line don't seem to be working all that well, do it love?'

'Claire, we has to persevere in our line of business. We'll have to get a bit tougher, that's all.'

'Lennie,' Claire said worriedly. 'I don't like you roughing people up. You know you got sent down last...'

'Shut it, will you! Just don't go on about it.' Lennie shouted. He strode to the door. 'Got to get the shop opened, see you later.' He turned to scowl at her. 'Just you go easy on the cash, eh!' The door closed behind him.

For a while Claire stared at the front door, then she turned to the mirror and pouted; why was he always going on about money? That shop would be a little gold mine with the prices he was charging. She tugged again at her hair, it definitely did need setting. As for Lennie, she would try not to worry, he'd be sure to fix everything.

Chapter Forty Three

Saturday afternoon

Simon finished making up the last of his flower orders and set them to one side at the back of the shop, his customers would collect them on their way home from town. He looked at his watch, soon be time to close. Then he walked over to the window and stood glaring at the shop across the road. The phone rang and he hurried to answer it.

'Simon Mitchell's florist,' he announced.

'It's me, Barry Downs, thought I'd let you know I'm at a petrol station on the Harrogate road now, just filling up, should be with you in about five minutes,'

'Great' Simon replied, 'I'll get the kettle on, but park your van on the back street. I've left the back door unlocked. You can come up through the garden.'

'Right you are. See you soon.' There came a click as the line disconnected.

Simon got some mugs and filled the kettle, it was freezing out there and Barry would be sure in need of a hot drink. Having done that he returned to look again out of the window and to stare at the line of Christmas trees, all stacked up against the wall of the shop across the road.

There were at least three dozen trees displayed outside the shop and people were milling around examining them. He resisted the urge to go across the road and look at them himself; that would be unprofessional, besides he could leave that to Barry. The kettle boiled and he went to make the tea. Just as he did so, the shop doorbell tinkled and he turned to see Mrs Roberts standing there.

'Sorry I'm a bit early,' she said, but for some reason I found a parking space easily today.' She looked around, 'Any sign of the grower yet?'

'Barry will be here in a couple of minutes.' Simon said. As he spoke he heard the faint sound of the back door opening and footsteps approaching. He turned to see Barry coming through the connecting door.

'Here you are then, punctual as ever,' Simon said.

'You know me Simon,' Barry said, 'I like to be on time.' He strode up to the shop window and looked out. 'This where they're flogging my trees then?' He asked. He made as if to go out through the shop door but Simon held him back.

'Hang on a minute. Even if they are your trees I don't want you to make any fuss just yet.' He guided him to where Mrs Roberts was standing. 'This lady is Mrs Roberts and she is going to help us with our enquiries.' Barry nodded and smiled politely at her.

'Nice to meet you, Barry.' Cynthia smiled as she shook his hand. 'Will you let me give you a little advice in case those trees turn out to be yours?'

Barry nodded and listened to her carefully.

'So now, you drink your tea.' Simon said as he gave him the mug. 'Then when you are ready, go have a look. If they're yours, don't cause any rumpus. Just come here through the back way again and we'll do the rest.

Barry drank his tea then scowled, 'You sure about this, Si? 'Cause my gut tells me they really are my trees. I want to wring that bloke's neck!'

'No! Barry. Leave that to us. Just come back and let us know.'

'Right,' growled Barry. 'Just as long as he gets what's coming.' With that he strode back through the connecting door.

Simon watched him go then explained to Mrs Roberts 'That bloke doesn't know who Barry is, but if he sees him coming from the shop entrance he might make the connection.'

They both looked out of the window and watched as Barry crossed the road and examined the trees outside the shop opposite. It didn't take long. Within a couple of minutes Barry, with a face like thunder, marched back across the road.

'No need to ask really,' Simon said, 'judging from his expression, we can see that they're his.' He looked at Mrs Roberts hopefully. 'Now what do we do?'

Mrs Roberts walked towards the shop door, opened it and looked out along the street. 'We wait for Miss Windle.'

*

Laura hurried along the High Street and tried not to feel irritated, she risked a hasty glance at her watch, 5.28pm. She knew it. She was going to be late. She would have been on time, had it not been for the fact that at the last minute she had had to take in a parcel for her next door neighbours as they had not yet returned from their Christmas shopping. Laura clicked her tongue in annoyance.

As she approached Mr Mitchell's shop, she thought about her appointment with Cynthia and wondered what it was that she wanted her to do. Better to try not to ask too many questions about Mrs Thackeray, she thought. Mr Collinson would surely tell her in good time. She reached the shop door. Now, concentrate woman, she told herself, and she went inside.

'I'm so sorry I'm late,' Laura began.

'Only by a minute,' Cynthia smiled.

Laura looked around and saw Mr Mitchell and another man standing slightly behind Cynthia. They both looked very serious.

'What has happened?' she enquired anxiously. 'Is something wrong?'

'Not to worry, Miss Windle.' Cynthia said. 'With your help, we're going to put it right.' She took hold of her arm and guided her towards the shop window. 'You see that new shop that's opened across the road?'

'I have heard about it. They opened up yesterday and they will be selling fancy goods and all that. Unfortunately, I have not had the time to look at it closely.' Laura peered through the window and frowned, 'Although it does look rather like they are also selling Christmas trees.' She turned to look at Simon Mitchell. 'I have to say, that is most inconsiderate of them.'

'Don't I know it?' Mr Mitchell muttered.

'You are right,' Cynthia said, 'and this is why Mr Mitchell and I want you to help us.'

Laura looked again at the grim expression on Simon Mitchell's face. She just hoped he had not got himself into trouble again. 'Of course, as long as it is legal?'

'It is,' Cynthia said. 'Now this is what we want you to do.'

*

Lennie Stones leaned against the shop door and watched the slight elderly lady examining the Christmas trees. He gave a weary sigh; she'd been poking around at them for the last ten minutes. It was a wonder that half the pine needles hadn't fallen off judging by the way she pulled and pushed at them. He took a last drag from his ciggie, then stamped out the butt on the floor and strode up to her. 'Afternoon young lady. Them's nice trees ain't they? Best value in Fawdon they is. I tell you what my darling, you could never get those Christmas trees in Kirkgate market at that price.'

The woman turned to glare at him. 'I am not a young lady, and I am certainly not your darling,' she replied. 'So please do not patronise me.' She picked out the smallest Christmas tree and held it up. 'How much is this one?'

'What it says on it, missus,' Lennie replied, '75p, and you'll not get it cheaper nowhere else.'

'That I can well believe.' She gave him the tree. 'I will take it.'

Lennie grinned and held out his hand. '75p please.'

'Could you please put some newspaper round its roots?' The woman followed him into the shop and watched him wrap the tree. She gave him the money.

'Ta,' Lennie said as he pushed the cash into his pocket.

'I would like a receipt please.' The woman said.

'What? Lennie stared at her, 'for a 75p? I promise you missus, no one's going to arrest you for shoplifting trees.'

'I need it for my records. It is for business so I must insist.'

'Oh all right then,' he grumbled. 'Your boss tight about money, is he?' He went behind the counter and scribbled out a receipt from a receipt book and signed it. 'This'll have to do, missus,' he muttered, 'me till's not working yet.'

She checked it. 'Thank you,' she said, then she picked up the tree and walked out of the shop.

Lennie stared after her. 'What an old fuss pot,' he muttered. Still, he'd always thought these Fawdoners were a weird lot. Anyway it was near time to close up. He started to bring the stock inside. He'd be glad when Christmas was over. He grinned, then the Fawdoners wouldn't see him for dust.

Chapter Forty Four

Sunday night
7pm

Martha and Cynthia stood in the ladies washroom of Lorenzo's Restaurant and put on their uniforms, then looked in the mirror. Martha buttoned up her white overall and picked up the tall chef's hat. 'Funny,' she said to Cynthia, 'I've always wanted to wear one of these.' She placed it on her head, squared her shoulders, and peered at her reflection. 'Makes me look much taller and impressive. All I need now is a wooden spoon.'

'And a kerchief round your neck,' Cynthia lisped, her mouth full of hair grips as she struggled to pin up her auburn curls. Having done so she turned to Martha. 'How do I look?'

Martha giggled, 'You look a bit like a Victorian school teacher.'

'That doesn't worry me,' Cynthia replied, 'I've looked like so many people in my time,' she said as she pinned the waitress's lacy cap into place. 'In fact, this outfit makes me look quite respectable.'

*

Alfredo smiled broadly as his new chef and waitress came into the restaurant. 'You two do look wonderful, I wish I always had staff that looked like you.'

'But can you afford us?' Cynthia grinned.

'And are we recognisable?' Martha asked

'Not unless someone looked at you closely,' Alfredo said, 'and as I intend only to use candlelight for the dining area tonight, I'll think we'll be alright,' he raised an eyebrow.

'That should help. I've already briefed Miss Windle about your plan,' Cynthia said.

Someone rapped on the restaurant door. 'I hope that this is an invited guest,' Alfredo said as he hurried to open it, 'I did put a private party notice on the door.'

Cynthia smiled when she saw that it was Neill who came in. She hurried to greet him as Alfredo helped him take off his overcoat.

'This is my friend Neill Collinson, Alfredo,' Cynthia said. 'I've told you about him?'

'Of course,' said Alfredo and shook Neill's hand warmly. 'And I thank you for your support in this.' He paused and looked at Neill's suit critically. 'So! You look the perfect waiter. What more could I wish for?'

'I wish I felt like the perfect waiter,' Neill replied nervously. 'I'm not that good an actor, just hope I don't spill the soup over someone's head.'

'Which reminds me,' Alfredo said, 'I'd better keep an eye on that.' He walked over to Martha and smiled. 'If you'll come with me, I'll show you where the dishes are kept.' He took her arm and they went towards the kitchen area.

*

Cynthia watched them walk away for a moment, then Neill said, 'They make a nice couple.'

'Indeed they do,' Cynthia replied, 'they seem just right for each other.' She touched Neill's arm. 'Still feeling nervy?'

He smiled and held her hand. 'I've never been employed as a waiter before.' He tugged at his bow tie. 'It's downright terrifying.'

Cynthia grinned, 'You've just got a bit of stage fright, that's all.'

'Stage fright or not, I just want to help you catch these villains.'

Cynthia looked at him thoughtfully, 'I'm really grateful that you came. I do appreciate this.' She saw that his face flushed at her words.

He stared at her and seemed about to say something, then he gave a self-conscious laugh and blurted, 'Don't worry my dear, my invoice is in the post.'

Cynthia bit down on her lip, disappointed at his reply. She looked at the floor. Have I got this wrong, she wondered? Did I misjudge that goodnight kiss last Saturday night? Maybe now that he's found the missing arsonist he has no further use for me. She felt a kind of sadness as she thought about this. Was their renewed friendship about to conveniently fizzle out after they had dealt with this case? She had to admit she hoped for something deeper. *Are you in love with him?* An inner voice asked. No! But the truth was she didn't know. She only knew that the second he came into the room her pulse began to quicken. Was that love?

'Why so thoughtful, Cynth?' Neill's voice reached her.

She smiled brightly, 'I'm just hoping all goes according to Alfredo's plan.' She watched as Alfredo went from table to table lighting the candles on each one of them. Then he walked back to the mains switch and turned off the electric lights. The result was charming. Now the restaurant was enveloped in a warm glow of candlelight. The aroma of wine and the scent of garlic mingled in the air in perfect harmony and in the background, romantic Italian music played softly.

'The scene is set and it looks fantastic.' Cynthia murmured.

'And so do you.' Neill whispered as he gazed at her.

Alfredo came up to and stood beside them. Then he smiled, 'All is in readiness,' he said. He looked at the restaurant door. 'Now we await the guests.'

*

Laura Windle was the first to arrive. She tapped hesitantly on the restaurant door then entered cautiously. 'Oh dear,' she said as Alfredo came to greet her, 'I do hope I am not too early?'

'On time to the minute, Miss Windle,' Alfredo said, 'if you'll follow me?' He led her to a table at the far end of the restaurant.

Neill also came to greet her. 'I want to thank you for your help, Miss Windle, in the arson case,' he said as he seated himself at her table, 'I'm sorry I didn't have the opportunity to talk to you before, but your assistance on that case was most appreciated.'

Laura looked at him, her grey eyes bright with interest. 'Then I was right? It was...?'

At that moment the restaurant door opened again and Peter Greystone, accompanied by his wife Helen, came in.

Neill jumped to his feet. 'I'm part-time waiter for tonight,' he explained hurriedly, 'I'll join you again later.'

Laura stared after him, she felt irritated. She would have dearly loved to know what had happened to Edna Thackeray, but then she checked herself – that is not the real reason why you are here. She thought about the blackmailers. Last Saturday Cynthia had told her that she was certain Claire Forbes was one of them. What would Julia have made of her baby sister's behaviour? She would surely have been incensed. As Laura thought about this she felt her face burn with shame. *But you are the root cause of all this, even though what you did in the first place was for a good reason* a small voice reminded her. 'Then I must do all that I can to put things right,' she murmured. Looking around the room, she peered closely at Alfredo's new chef and waitress and smiled, then she nodded politely at Peter Greystone and his wife as they came into the restaurant. Toying idly with the clasp of her handbag she remembered Cynthia's instructions. When the time was right she knew exactly what she had to do.

The restaurant door opened again and the strident voice of Claire Forbes was heard complaining loudly. 'See, I told you we'd be late, the card said 7pm and look, other folks has got here before us.'

'It's only five minutes and they won't have eaten everything up by now,' argued her escort, a tall smartly dressed man with a voice like gravel. 'Here,' he said as he looked round, 'what's with all the candles then? What's the betting the Italian's not paid his electric bill?'

'Will you shush, Lennie,' Claire said as she saw Alfredo approaching. 'Here he comes now. I'm sorry we're late,' she began.

'Don't you dare blame me,' Lennie interrupted, 'she couldn't stop fussing with her hair.'

'It looks splendid to me, you must have an excellent hairdresser,' Alfredo said. 'So, if you will follow me?' He led them to a table opposite Miss Windle and seated them. 'Welcome to my restaurant,' then with a brief nod he returned to the kitchen.

*

Peter Greystone watched the blonde woman and the lanky man seat themselves at the table opposite Miss Windle. It was hard to see their features clearly in this light but he felt sure that he had heard that female voice somewhere before.

'Pity about the lighting,' Helen, his wife murmured, 'no one can see my lovely new shoes.'

'You can show them off some other time,' Peter said distractedly as he looked around the room. He saw that several of the other tables had a reserved card on them, but that there were only five other guests present, apart from the staff of course. His gaze moved on, taking in the drifting swirls of smoke from the candles, the deep crimson of the small roses that adorned each table, the glint of silver from the cutlery. Funny how candlelight enhanced metal. He looked at the gold necklace that the blonde woman was wearing, how it shimmered in this light, even the man's silver wristwatch strap gleamed brightly. Something niggled at the back of his mind. What was it? It couldn't be Helen's new shoes, she'd babbled on about them all the way here. He stared at Alfredo. Should he have remembered something? Another question came into his mind – why had they been invited? Then a shrill laugh from the blonde's table interrupted his train of thought and he glowered at her in irritation, before staring down at the cutlery in front of him.

What was it he'd been thinking about? Something about metal? About silver? Slowly his gaze returned to the wristwatch the blonde's escort was wearing. He scowled. What the hell was it about that bloody watch?

It was bothering him. He sold lots of that type every year.

'Why are you scowling at everyone?' Helen hissed, 'you know you're supposed to smile at people, especially when they invite you to a free dinner.'

'It's just…' He broke off as a bowl of minestrone soup was placed in front of him, then he stared open mouthed up at the waitress. Was he hallucinating? Or was he seeing Cynthia Roberts?

The waitress smiled, placed a finger to her lips and walked away.

Peter sat up straight, his mind now on red alert. Something was going on in here tonight, but he didn't know what. He squinted again at the other couple also seated at the far end of the restaurant. He did not recognise the man and although he could not see the woman's face, as her back was turned towards him, he knew it was Miss Windle. She had greeted them earlier when they came into the restaurant.

'Will you stop staring at people?' Helen whispered.

'But, don't you see…'

'Just drink your soup.' Helen insisted, then as she tasted it, 'hmm, quite delicious.'

Dutifully Peter picked up his spoon and sipped his soup, but he had lost all sense of taste. He watched as a stern faced Alfredo approached the blonde's table and placed a gleaming silver dish in front of the couple.

'What's all this?' he heard the man ask.

With a flourish, Alfredo lifted the lid.

'Bloody Hell! Mushrooms!' The man shouted. 'Is this some kind of joke?'

'Some of these are good. Some of these are poisonous, just like you.' Alfredo said. 'Now eat!'

'Ere,' screeched the blonde, 'we're not eating that. We're not trying to poison nobody.'

Alfredo loomed over them, his face dark with anger. 'But the letters you sent trying to blackmail people were. You sent them to people who had already paid the price. You are bloodsuckers and the evil you do is poison.'

The man laughed contemptuously. 'You stupid fool,' he said, 'prove it.'

Cynthia Roberts joined Alfredo at the table. 'You are right,' she said. 'We can't prove that you sent those letters to the people here.'

'See,' sneered the blonde.

'But we have evidence that you, Mr. Lennie Stones, sell stolen goods in your shop.' She beckoned to Miss Windle. 'And Miss Windle here can prove it.'

'Indeed I can,' Miss Windle said. She walked to their table, opened her handbag, and brought out the receipt for a Christmas tree.

Lennie looked at it, 'Who's gonna believe that old biddy?' he sneered.

Claire nudged him, 'That's Miss Windle, my sister's friend. Don't you recognise her from before?' She hissed.

'So it is,' Lennie said, 'but then old biddies all look the same to me.' He looked around at the other diners then said loudly. 'You can all blame her and her pal, Julia, Claire's big sister.' He heard Miss Windle gasp then added. 'For years they've been keeping records on the wrong-doings of you Fawdoners, it was going to be a nice little earner.' He turned to look at Claire, 'but then her big sister went and got herself killed. So, end of story, except Claire thought that the records might still be there, so I decided to have a look-see.'

'You burgled my house!' Miss Windle gasped in outrage. She turned to face the others, 'Yes, I did have records in my house, also some information from Claire's sister. But I can assure all of you they would never have seen the light of day.' She glared at Lennie, 'And now I shall burn them.'

'Believe that if you like, I wouldn't,' Lennie sneered. He stood up and took Claire's arm, pulling her to him.

'The police have been informed that you are selling stolen goods. They have seen the evidence and are on their way.' Alfredo said.

'No chance,' said Lennie. He pulled Claire in front of him and began to back towards the restaurant door.

Alfredo attempted to grab him then stepped back instantly when Lennie produced a gun.

'One move from any of you lot and I'll use it.' Lennie said as he pointed the gun at them. Holding Claire as a shield in front of him, they edged step by step towards the door. 'I'm not getting sent down again. I'll see you all in hell first.' Abruptly he staggered backwards over Peter's well placed leg and fell to the ground.

The gun went off, the bullet hitting the ceiling. Instantly Peter was straddling him, pushing the weapon across the floor. 'You! You lousy southpaw with your watch on your right hand. I should have known, you bastard. You were the bloke who clobbered me at Mallins mill. Now it's your turn.'

'I can hear a police siren,' Cynthia Roberts said.

'Get back, the lot of you,' Claire said coldly. Unnoticed by the others she'd picked up the gun. 'And you,' she said, addressing Peter, 'get off him.' She looked down at Peter. 'Now'! She insisted, 'or I'll shoot.'

Holding his hands high Peter climbed off Lennie as the sound of a police siren grew louder. Claire pulled Lennie to his feet. 'Don't try anything you lot, just stand clear.' She waved the gun warningly. 'Come on Lennie... run!' With that, they raced through the door.

Neill and Peter made as if to go after them but Cynthia stopped them. 'They won't go far,' she said. 'They both have records and the police know where Claire lives.' As she spoke the police officers came into the restaurant.

Alfredo hurried over to them, told them what had happened and warned them that the couple were armed.

The officer nodded and went to phone the station.

When the police had gone Alfredo turned towards his guests,

'Please everyone, return to your tables. The police will deal with those villains now. So come, let us enjoy the rest of our meal together.'

*

'Move it! Move it. Come on you lazy cow.' Lennie yelled as he pushed past Claire, racing out on to the street ahead of her and towards his car.

'I can't run fast in these shoes,' Claire whined.

'Then take 'em off, stupid.' Lennie shouted as he opened the car door and jumped in.

'Don't go without me,' Claire pleaded as she heard the engine start up. She hobbled to the car door and managed to jump in just as the car sped off.

'What'll we do now then, Lennie?' she gasped, 'we could go home?'

Lennie looked at her, 'Are you flaming mad or what? They know where you live, woman! The cops are probably sat outside waiting for us.'

The sound of a police siren grew louder and Lennie, looking in the car mirror, could see the flashing blue light. He pressed his foot down hard on the accelerator.

Claire grabbed his arm, 'Where we going then?'

Lennie looked again in the mirror, 'They're getting too close. We need to lose them.' He glanced at Claire, 'You still got that gun?'

'You want me to kill them?'

'No! You moron. Just wind down the car window and aim for the tyres.'

'But what if...?'

'Just bloody well do it!'

Claire opened the window, aimed the gun and squeezed the trigger. There came a loud 'crack,' a squeal of brakes and the police car behind them skidded to one side and stopped.

'Yippee!' shouted Lennie.

'Did I hit the tyres?'

'No,' Lennie laughed, 'but you blasted all hell out of their windscreen. That's them out of the way for now.'

'I didn't kill anybody did I?' Claire whispered anxiously.

'How the hell would I know?' Lennie grinned. He looked at her with contempt. 'It's you that fired the gun.' He pressed down hard again on the accelerator.

'Where we going now?'

'I'm heading for the M1, best thing is to go south for London, get out of the way of these local cops.'

Ten minutes later Lennie began to relax, now they were about to leave the Rothwell road and join the M1. Everything would be fine once he reached London. He knew a few mates there. He stared through the windscreen as he approached the slip road then cursed furiously in disbelief. Two police cars with flashing lights blocked the entrance to the motorway.

'What's wrong?' Claire said.

'Looks like we're finished, girl' Lennie said. He gave a deep sigh, switched off the engine and watched the policemen approaching. 'I forgot that police cars have radio.'

Epilogue

April 1973

Simon Mitchell wiped the sweat from his brow and tried hard not to panic. There were bouquets everywhere, all neatly labelled and all due to be delivered before Good Friday. Only the delivery man had just phoned in and told him he was down with the flu. What was he to do? There was nothing else for it, he would have to wait until closing time and deliver the bouquets himself. Which meant of course, he'd be late for supper unless he popped into the village chip shop? That would just have to do.

Later that evening, as he parked the van and delivered a bouquet to Number 22 Westdown Road, he noticed the 'For Sale' sign in the garden of Julia Barnes' old house next door. He stared up at it and felt puzzled. He had heard all about Mrs Barnes kid sister who had inherited that house, and the dreadful scandal she and her boyfriend were involved in. Of course he'd known that her boyfriend was a crook, and he'd certainly not got away with pinching Barry's Christmas trees. Mrs Roberts had sorted that alright. But, Simon wondered, the frightening thing was that he had heard that the boyfriend had threatened Alfredo with a gun. Was that just gossip? The sensible thing to do would be to wait until the real truth came up at the trial. Still, it was worrying the things that people got up to.

He shook his head and got back in his van, some folk were strange. Most people liked it here in Fawdon. His thoughts turned towards Edna Thackeray and the letter he'd received from her in February. She'd told him that the police investigation had cleared her of all charges and that her husband's cousin had been charged with libel. She'd also said she'd not be returning to Fawdon but that she hoped that she could visit him one day?

Simon had felt sad at this. He'd enjoyed being looked after and Edna was such a nice woman. At first he'd sat down and started to write to her, but then he'd hesitated and put down his pen. Did he really want Edna back? True she had been cleared as nothing could be proved but, deep down, did he really want to risk it? After all it would not only be his premises at stake, but his livelihood too. What on earth would become of him if his shop were to be burned down?

His head had ruled his heart and finally he'd written her a friendly note telling her that she would be more than welcome to come and they would spend a day in town together. There, he thought, no one could be offended at that, and it would be the end of the matter.

He looked up at the 'For Sale' sign again as he drove off – it could well be a good investment. As for its former owner, he could distinctly remember selling some pink geraniums to the lady for her front garden, but that had been last winter. He smiled, it was early days yet, but soon he would need to plan for his retirement and buying a house in Fawdon might not be a bad idea.

*

Saturday Morning

Cynthia Roberts pulled back the curtains and stared glumly out at the rain and mist. Are we ever going to see some sunshine again, she wondered. She yawned and stretched and went back into the kitchen to make herself some toast. She felt a slight sense of guilt as she had taken a Saturday morning off before the Easter break, when really she should have been in her office catching up on paper work.

She shrugged. All in all, this year had started off well. She'd managed to sort out the blackmailing villains, as well as dealing with the theft of Christmas trees. The fees from the blackmail cases, and the publicity that had followed the theft case, had certainly not done her any harm. Especially when the Yorkshire Post newspaper published a large photo and an article on Mr. Mitchell and her with the heading, *Fawdon P.I. solves the case of the stolen Christmas trees.* The result was that now she had several cases on her books, one for a missing person and several divorce cases. Not to mention the mystery of three lost dogs and one pet goat, all who independently seemed to have vanished without a trace.

Sipping her coffee she walked back to the window and looked out again. She would have to go to the supermarket soon to buy some groceries for the long weekend. Neill had phoned last night and they'd planned, weather permitting, to take a trip out to Scarborough on the Sunday or Monday, just to get a breath of sea air. She thought about Neill and smiled. Just where was their relationship heading? Neill wanted a much more serious commitment, he had not as yet mentioned the 'marriage' word, but she felt sure that he would ask her one day. She sighed, she still needed time and she still thought about her Harry. Would it then be right to marry Neill and then compare him to Harry, in her mind that seemed most unfair?

Another problem crept into her mind. Should she tell Neill about her dark past? If she did so how would he react? Would his attitude change? Or would he just walk away?

She gave an inpatient sigh, walked over to the sink and put her cup on the draining board. Enough with the worries, it was time to treat herself. She'd kept to her diet over these last six months, but now she had seen exactly what she wanted for a reward. She slipped on her raincoat and went out of the door. There was a huge chocolate Easter egg in the sweet shop near the supermarket and, for once, she was going to indulge. After all, she told herself, one of the best things about Easter were the Easter eggs.

It had been a cold and rainy spring and Laura was busy packing to go to Majorca with a group from the Women's Institute for the Easter holidays. Her thoughts drifted back to the last time she had visited the beautiful island over two years ago and she smiled in anticipation. Of course back then her friend Julia, had looked after Snowy, her cat, but since Julia had passed away... Laura bit down on her lip as she thought about Julia. It was true she had been annoying at times, but she still missed her. Now Snowy would have to stay in a cattery. Laura felt a bit uneasy about this but she knew the owners of the cattery and she was sure that Snowy would be well looked after. She consoled herself with the thought that she would only be away for two weeks.

Think of something cheerful, she told herself as she started to write out the luggage labels. Think of the lovely Lawry Hotel that she had been to on her last visit to Majorca. Back then, she and the other ladies had been invited there for cocktails, but this time they had been invited for a gala dinner – that really would be wonderful.

As she tied the labels on to the handles of the cases she thought about the nightmare weeks she had endured last winter, especially the weeks before Christmas. Thankfully Claire Forbes and her blackmailing villain of a boyfriend had been arrested and they had been charged not only for theft, but for attempted bodily harm, damage to a police vehicle and, most alarmingly, for the illegal possession of a fire arm.

Laura wondered what had become of Edna Thackeray. Was she really a pyromaniac? Laura doubted it. Still, she had not been seen on Mr Mitchell's premises since early December. She had, of course, politely enquired as to her whereabouts, but Mr Mitchell had been somewhat vague in his reply. Still, she thought, the truth would come out eventually; everything did in time.

The truth came out about you, didn't it? An inner voice said. *It's not as if you were perfect.* Laura felt her face flush as she remembered the dreadful accusations that Lennie had made. The awful thing was that some of it was true. She remembered going home that night and getting out her ledger and the copies of notes on prospective clients and burning them the very next morning. So, everything was gone now, all turned into ashes. All would be forgotten. Or would it? Laura frowned; yes, she must try to forget what she knew but how does one forget what is so clearly etched into one's memory? Surely it is well-nigh impossible to erase such things and, a little knowledge is a dangerous thing. Her thoughts turned towards Cynthia Roberts and she smiled in approval; that young woman had done really well, she'd dealt with the blackmailers and with the case of the theft of the Christmas trees superbly. Now it seemed that after such a dark past, Cynthia was finally well on the road to success in her new career. Surely now nothing could go wrong?

Laura wished her well and she felt proud that Cynthia had asked for her help. For a while her life had been so exciting and now it was over. She thought about that and felt a little sad. 'Cheer up and finish your packing, woman,' she told herself sternly. 'Spring is here, you are going on holiday without any more guilt or anxiety. You don't need to worry about the vicar, nor do you need to be concerned about Mrs Mould's drinking problems, well at least not for a fortnight. When you return you will have the summer to look forward to. She went downstairs to her desk and got out her passport and currency. All was as it should be. Smiling, she placed them in her handbag, picked up her coat, then walked over the window to await her taxi.

Also by Eileen Robertson:
We'll be Watching You

Published by:
Robert Hale (in hardback) 2013;
Harlequin (In paperback) 2014

Christine Brett has two problems, one her disempowering divorce and two, caring for her invalid mother Emily. Matters don't improve when Christine becomes obsessed with the Neighbourhood Watch and reports her neighbours for trivial offences. This infuriates Harry Myers, a neighbour, and a row breaks out.

On the next day Christine boycotts the local shops and visits the supermarket. It is there that she witnesses a robbery. She sees the face of the getaway driver, he seems strangely familiar. She becomes frightened when she reports what she's seen to the police and discovers that her reputation of 'crying wolf' has preceded her and no one appears to take her seriously.

As she returns home Christine's fear grows when she realizes that if she can identify the getaway driver, he has also seen her. And that as she's the sole witness he will do his utmost to silence her.

Review by Joanna Patrick

I really enjoyed this. It reminded me a little of 'The Hundred-Year-Old Man who Climbed out of the Window and disappeared,' although I actually preferred this book. Great pace, fantastic sense of humor and lovely interplay between the characters – particularly Christine and Emily. I won't say anything more, in case I give too much away.

Review by Kaz Clark

Yet again Eileen Robertson has penned another cosy crime page turner, and it's every bit as good as her previous novels. I love the way she brings to life her characters, the way she draws you in deeper and deeper with a clever plot and believable dialogue all wrapped around a thread of rib tickling humour. Who says crime doesn't pay? It certainly has for this entertaining author. I can't wait for her next book.

Also by Eileen Robertson:
Miss McGuire is Missing

When Ben Hammond reluctantly embarks on a pensioners coach tour, he is surprised to find that he has met one of his fellow passengers before. It is Miss McGuire, his former maths teacher and she is acting rather strangely. On the journey home, Ben realises that Miss McGuire is no longer on the coach, but when he is told that she is visiting her sister, alarm bells start ringing; Miss McGuire has no sister. Ben feels compelled to investigate, and when he does he unearths all manner of dark secrets. Suspicious characters lurk in the gloom of the Full Moon Inn, and at a nursing home nearby elderly people are disappearing...

Praise for 'Miss McGuire is Missing'

"Miss McGuire is Missing" has all the ingredients I love: Mystery, suspense, humour. A brilliant first novel and I can't wait to read her next one."
   -Raymond Allen, author of 'Some Mothers Do 'Ave Em.'

"No Sleep with this page turner from Eileen Robertson, I can't wait to read her next one."
   -June Hampson, author of 'Fighting Dirty'

"A well-written mystery that will entertain you and keep you guessing"
   -Catherine King, author of 'The Orphan Child'

"It's a roller-coaster of a yarn as the intrepid trio discover that not only Miss McGuire is missing.'
   - Roberta Grieve, Novelist, 'The Woman Writer' Magazine

Also by Eileen Robertson: Blackmail for Beginners

Published by Robert Hale
ISBN: 978-0-7090-9381-7

Review by Lizzie Hayes

Laura Windle is a retired teacher, now taking an active part in village life. A supporter of good causes, she fund-raises for the children's hospital. When she is advised that the expected funds fall short of the amount required to pay for a young boy's life-saving treatment, she decides that she must take action.

A little investigation establishes that the pledges of money from three of the town's better-off citizens have not been honoured. So Laura decides that she must persuade the recalcitrant three that they should honour their promises. Having spent her working life keeping an eagle eye on the children in her care, nothing gets past Laura who now has an abundance of information at her disposal to coerce her reluctant contributors.

We follow the lives of the three unwilling pledgers, as a visit from Laura Windle drops like a bomb on their already complicated lives. Each of them has problems and now additionally they have Laura Windle.

This is a wonderful story of village life and questionable ethics, as in the interests of saving a young life Laura Windle turns to blackmail. Whilst wriggling on the hook, the three victims attempt to evade Laura's justice, but her main problem comes from an unexpected source which brings startling consequences.

A delightful tale. I look forward to the next.

This review has previously appeared on Lizzie Hayes's blog Promoting Crime Fiction, March 2012, and in the April issue of Mystery People magazine.

Made in the USA
Charleston, SC
11 February 2016